C000142616

A HEART THAT LOVES

Book Four: A Heart that Dances Series

J.P. STERLING

© Copyright 2022

All Rights Reserved. Unauthorized duplication or distribution is strictly prohibited.

J.P. Sterling

Copy Editor: Lawrence Editing

Developmental Editor: David Brooks

All rights reserved. With the exception of brief quotations in review-with proper accreditation-no part of this publication may be reproduced or transmitted in any form or by any means, electronic or mechanical, including photocopying, recording, or by any information storage and retrieval system, without the prior written permission from the author, except where permitted by law. Contact the author for information on foreign rights.

This book is fiction and for entertainment purposes only. Any mention of places, people or events is fictional.

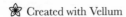 Created with Vellum

Author Notes

Thank you for your interest in A Heart that Loves.
A special gift for you:
Listen to FREE Audio Books written by J.P. Sterling on
her YouTube Channel https://www.youtube.com/
channel/UCA9sy4oLZhT8Iffqg8KAHhA

Chapter One

**"She was like the moon – part of her was
always hidden away."**— Dia Reeves

They say you never forget your first love. The one who
got away . . . As happy as I was in my place in life—the
path I never took haunted me. Only my first love was
never about a person, but about my art—ballet. I felt I
was suspended in between two worlds: one being the
world I had dreamed of and the other the one I just sort
of hap-hazardly wandered into after being thrown from
my dream world. Don't get me wrong. I'm immensely
grateful for the opportunity that I have now, but as I
walked to work this morning, I found myself wondering:
what if I'd gone another way? I know my health condition
made being a professional ballerina impossible, but there
had to be something else . . . While my thoughts flowed,

one of my favorite dance memories pulled to the front of my mind.

It had been my freshman year and my ballet company was casting for The Nutcracker. I missed out on the role of Clara that I mistakenly thought I had been a shoe-in for. My dance rival, Erica got the part by a landslide. The judges cited her as being lighter on her feet. I—to my astonishment—was cast as the Evil Mouse King. A definite blow to my ego at first, I stubbornly put my chin down and learned the steps. Then something magical happened. Somewhere between the steps, I discovered that even though it wasn't what I had wanted, I found another way to enjoy my favorite ballet. *It was a path unseen, but once taken, it was beautiful.* This was an early lesson for me to see that if something doesn't work out the way you had dreamed, maybe you can achieve it from a different viewpoint.

So this was what I pondered on my way to work, but it didn't slow me down. Having honed a talent for always being able to arrive at my workplace at the exact minute the clock turned to 8:00 a.m., today was no different as I breezed through the front door, and beelined right to the conference room where I knew Wally and Fulton were already waiting on me. Before I even had a chance to sit, I reached into my bag and pulled out a sheet I had prepared. With a playful smirk on my face, I pushed the one-page play synopsis across the table, perfectly landing it right in front of Wally and then I sank down into my chair and waited for a reaction. I tapped my foot exactly two times before Wally perked an eyebrow. "So, you titled the play, *A Purrrfect Valentine's Day.*"

Feeling the eagerness bud in my chest, I leaned closer, trying to rally him into my excitement. "It's going to be a playoff of '101 Dalmatians' but instead of puppies, we'll use cats. The hook will be" —I paused and made an arc above my head to resemble an imaginary banner— "A Love-hating-greedy-hag, who's trying to steal all the cats so people can't have them for pets."

"And by cats, you mean ballerinas?" Wally inquired.

"No." I doubled down. "I mean cats."

Wally raised the synopsis up, now concealing the front of his face as he read further and although I couldn't see what his facial expressions were doing, I did hear him snicker, so I knew he hadn't totally tossed the idea out. Just when I was about to claim victory, he lowered the page back down. "You can't put one hundred cats on a stage without having a *cat*astrophe."

"Why not?" I asked a little defensively.

Fulton cut in, "Cats can be aggressive and aren't trainable like dogs. Seriously if you put all those cats in the same room, they'll kill each other."

"Well . . ." I struggled to think on my feet. "What if I had ballerinas carry the cats across the stage as part of one of their dance interludes so the cats won't be free to intermix?"

"Where are we going to get that many cats?" Wally asked, with more of an air of intrigue than doubt. The thing I had learned about Wally was that he was just as creative as I was—if not more—and he was definitely more daring, so he was usually willing to hash out my most far-out ideas. In fact, he was crazy enough to go along with most of them if they didn't cost a lot of money.

I held up my finger as I continued to clarify my position. "This is the best part because it's a marketing dream. We are going to borrow them from the city shelters. We'll make a beautiful program with all their names, their adoption information, and adorable pictures. It will be our Valentine's charity mission to find these cats homes."

Wally and Fulton exchanged a look that said they were both amazed that this was making as much sense as it did. I knew Wally would eat up the idea of collabing with the shelters because it was adding publicity, but I could see from the narrowing in his eyes, he still had reservations and it was evident in his on-going questions. "So," Wally started again, "where is the plot going and why does she want to steal all the cats?"

"She owns a robot company and just launched robotic cats," I explained. "They are high tech AI, but they also catch mice and kids can play with them. Plus, the owners won't have the mess of a litter box or the expense of having to buy food. Most importantly—because she hates love and anything to do with it—she wants to void the world of anything capable of snuggling and giving people love. However, people don't buy her robot cats as well as she had planned, so she devises a plan to create a shortage of real cats so desperate parents will buy her robots for their kids as a stopgap."

"Okay . . ." Wally's face was pinched in a way I

knew I still had some convincing to do. "How are you going to end this?"

"So picture how it's going to be a dark and gloomy Valentine's Day with these scary robots that have cat fangs. The stage is going to be all creepy, but the hag is happy, with an evil giggle. Then we'll have to add in the usual Cupid-like person." I gestured with my hand to indicate I was taking an aside and said, "This is where the ballerina comes in and she uses her cupid powers to make Hag fall in love and she is instantly nice again, causing her to eventually go around and hand-deliver the cats to all the kids in town."

"Did you skip a part?" Wally asked. "Who are you going to get to fall in love with that hag? She sounds horrible."

"Maybe someone at the robot factory?" Fulton suggested.

"Nah," I immediately disagreed. "I think anyone at the robot factory is going to be in cohorts with her, not?"

Wally rocked on the back legs of his chair, the way the boys in grade school used too. It made me nervous, thinking he was going to crash backwards, but I also took it as a sign that he was thinking and evidently it paid off because he agreed. "Probably. We need to find someone else she is forced to be in association with."

I smiled a sly smile, knowing that all my planning efforts were about to pay off in a big way. "I already have it planned out." Holding up my pointed finger, I popped my eyes open wide, with one corner focused squarely on Fulton. "How about an adorable vet?"

Fulton's brow peaked; his eyes instantly cautioned

like he wasn't sure why I was buttering him up with the comparison. Then he took a guess as to why. "If you think I'm getting up on that stage, you're nuts."

"Oh no." I brushed his concern away. "We can find someone from the acting school to play the part." Still, I leaned a measure closer because I was trying to dig in hard to pull them in. "Don't you think it fits? Like the cats could maybe have ringworm or something nasty. She doesn't care about the cats, but the disease is contagious, and they infect her. She then becomes desperate to make them better, so she calls the vet. He ends up being adorably sweet to her even though she doesn't deserve it. He gives her medicine, but while she sleeps, the Cupids—played by ballerinas—switch her meds with a special 'deworming' pill that also gets rid of greed, and she falls in love and poof—"

"Poof, she poops out the hate," Wally interjected, stretching his lips wide across his face.

"Not like that," I scolded. "That would be gross, but you get my point. This is a starting point, and we can play around with it."

Wally was uncharacteristically silent for way too long. I was approaching that moment when I was ready to steal my synopsis back and rip it up because I knew I had disappointed him, but he saved me from having to be dramatic by saying, "I don't *hate* it. It's not the worst idea we've used."

"So, is that a yes?" I fished.

"It seems like a huge project for this little theatre," Wally thought out loud. "Although, I do like the idea of doing an adoption auction to work with the shelters. It seems things always go well when you add charity to them." He raised his eyes up to meet me, and I could tell by the gleam that even though he was reluctant, he was getting ready to give it his stamp of approval. "We can def play with the script and see where it goes."

About to breathe victory—because I could totally work with that—I kept my face flat, knowing there was still one logistical hurdle I needed to conquer, and like it was on cue, Wally tipped his head toward Fulton. "Why did Fulton need to be here?"

"I was about to ask the same thing but I'm sort of dreading it," Fulton said.

I innocently batted my lashes—perfectly layered in two coats of mascara—toward Fulton. "You can help write in the technical parts of the vet, but you also have connections to the shelters—"

"You want me on cat duty." He glared at me playfully.

"Maybe." I glared back just as playfully. "Depends. Would you do it?"

"You want me to coordinate a hundred cats?"

"No." I winked. "I want you to coordinate one hundred and *one* cats."

His eyes fled to the floor like he was looking for a secret trap door out of this conversation and he must've not seen one because after a short moment, he conceded and raised his gorgeous light green eyes back to meet mine, then said, "I'd love too."

"I knew you would." I smirked at him—a little sassy at first but I made sure to soften my smile so he could see how grateful I truly was that he was being so supportive of my super unreasonable request. "You're going to be amazing," I continued to butter him up.

"I can't think of anything else I'd rather do," he said sarcastically but I could also tell by the way he kept his eyes latched to mine that he was being a tiny bit honest in his enthusiasm to help me out.

Then, just like my dad used to wrap up his sales pitches, I homed in on how I was going to sell this script to Wally's customers. "This year's going to be tough because there's so much other live entertainment in the city and people haven't been spending as much money as they usually do on this sort of thing. I think it's going to be great to lean in and pull all our marketing efforts on how we are partnering with shelters to find homes for these cats in a sharing the love sort of mission. It'll give us a huge leg up over the competition."

"We can try it." Wally finally sounded convinced. "When do you think you can have a first draft of the script?"

"Well." I scratched the back of my head as I tried to think of something clever to say but when nothing came to me, I pulled out the one-hundred-page first draft I had stashed in my bag underneath the table. "You can have it now." I let my lips slide easily over my teeth in a giant upward curve. "I mean, I'll have to add the few adjustments and the ending we just talked about, but other than that, it is mostly laid out."

While his eyes skimmed the first page, he asked, "What would you have done if I would had said no?"

I shrugged, doing my best to convey a mysterious

vibe. "I might—or might not—have another option prepared for you."

Wally lowered a suspicious brow toward me in pause before leaning casually over toward Fulton and stated, "She's good."

"She's the best," Fulton agreed, while beaming in affirmation right at me, unleashing that heart-stopping boyish grin that seemed to always make my knees weak. It only lasted a moment, but it was long enough for me to feel lost because when it was over and I was forced to recoil my brain back to the present, I had completely forgotten what I was even talking about. Lucky for me, I quickly laid eyes on my script and remembered I was supposed to be wrapping up a creative meeting.

"On that note" –I stood up, collecting my bag and coffee mug— "I'm starving, and you have a script to read." I motioned to Wally.

Fulton pushed his chair back, standing up too, and asked, "Do you want to grab brunch or something before I have to go back to campus?"

"Don't you have some shelter calls to make?"

"I think I can manage that after I eat." Fulton's quick acceptance of my request only succeeded in making me grin larger—I seriously had to be the luckiest girl to have a boyfriend who would put up with all this stuff.

"In that case, of course." I lightheartedly linked arms with him—and without words because we didn't even need to ask where we'd eat—we headed outside to find our favorite food cart for lunch. It became our weekly tradition to hang out on the sidewalk and eat pork on a stick together as we mused about random things. It wasn't glamorous, but it was my favorite part of my week. After spending a year away from the city, eating amazing cuisine from a food truck on the side of the road was one of those things I had quickly learned to treasure.

Just as we passed through the line, I heard my phone ring in my purse and I promptly pulled it out, expecting it to be Gabby—who had told me she was going to call this week—but instead it was an out-of-state number I didn't recognize. "Hello," I said, a little distracted as I craned my neck to make sure Fulton wasn't stealing a bite from my pork stick.

"Is this Aubergine White?" a deep man's voice asked.

"Yes." I trod cautiously, wondering what this telemarketer was going to try to sell me, regretting that I hadn't silenced the call.

"This is the Richmond Police Department."

"Oh?" My interest was piqued now, and I repositioned the phone to be even more aligned with my ear. "What can I help you with?"

"We're calling to see if you have a location on Claire White?"

"That's my mom."

"Yes," he confirmed.

"She lives in Richmond. Well, she should," I added, feeling my uneasy gut feeling creep in. "Do you know something about her?" I squeaked out the question, but I already knew he wouldn't be calling unless he, in fact, did know something about her and my conscious was screaming at me that this was going to be bad—really, really bad.

"Yes, she set fire to her condo this morning and it spread, taking out half the houses on her block—"

I screamed. "What?" My hand flew over my mouth, covering my disbelief and then I stuttered, "I-Is she okay?"

"That's what we are trying to find out. It seems that we aren't able to locate her."

"Is everyone else okay?" My voice was shaky.

"Everyone is fine, thankfully."

I stared forward, unable to focus clearly on any one thing. "I don't believe it."

Fulton lightly touched my arm. "What's going on?"

Rotating the phone a slight angle away from my mouth, I whispered, "My mom set fire to her condo this morning and blew up half the town."

His naturally groomed eyebrows lifted, confirming he heard my words, but he respectfully stayed mute. The officer on the line interrupted, "Well, not half the town but several houses."

I held my forehead, feeling my head want to hang low from the instant shame that filled my heart. "I'm so sorry. What can I do to help you?" I managed as I fumbled for words.

"We'd like you to help us find your mother."

"Of course. I don't know anything, but I can help you brainstorm," I offered, still flabbergasted. Of all the stunts my mom had pulled, and there had been many— too many to recount—this had to be the most grandiose. After a quick exchange of information and an appointment to have a formal interview, I hung up the phone, looked at Fulton for support, and begged, "What am I going to do?" I didn't even have to ask or make a motion, but Fulton held his arms open wide, and I walked forward right into them, my forehead resting right under his chin, and I repeated, "What am I going to do now?"

"I guess we find a fugitive."

It was one of those things that should have made me cry, but it was so far beyond bad that I could only receive his comment as humorous and let out a nervous giggle. Taking one small step back so I didn't have to crane my neck all the way back to look up at him, I said, "I think I'd rather take my chances with a pile of one hundred cats."

Fulton held up a finger. "One hundred and *one*."

"Totally easier than this," I said, feeling a blank stare take over my face.

Fulton reached for my hand and squeezed it. "I'll help you. She can't be that far."

"Thank you," I said, completely overwhelmed to even begin to think about where to look for her. However, even though it seemed cliché, I did feel better knowing Fulton had voiced his support because I knew I was going to need all the help I could get.

Chapter
Two

"Hey, Becky." I answered my phone the next afternoon.

"Are you busy?"

"I am." I quickly saved the script I was editing, then closed out the screen. "But I can take a break. What's up?"

"I didn't hear you leave this morning and I got up super early, so I was surprised you were already gone. I guess . . . I was wondering if you're okay."

I sighed heavily, slumping way down into my desk chair. "I was up all night. My head wouldn't shut off, so I accidentally ended up planning all the music for our Valentine's production. Then I decided to get started on the choreography, but I didn't want to stomp around and make a bunch of noise to wake you, so I came to the theatre early."

Becky let out one of her tiny giggles that always reminded me more of the Pillsbury doughboy than of a prep-school girl like Becky. "Like you could ever stomp around. You're the most light-footed person I know."

"Phish, then you haven't seen me try to get some of these sequences out. I'm definitely not as nimble as I used to be."

"I'm sure you are being too hard on yourself."

"I don't know about that."

Then there was a pause in the conversation, and I knew Becky was getting ready to pry and almost on cue, she gently asked, "So . . . have you heard from your mom?"

"Nope." I subconsciously tucked my free arm across my chest. "I don't expect to either. She has never run *to* me. It's always away from me."

"It's super scary, though, because she could be hurt."

"I know." My voice was soft, like words would damage my throat. I knew Becky was thinking I was wrought with stress over my mom's ordeal—and I think a normal person would have been—but the truth of the matter was that I was numb to it. Once I got over the initial shock of the fire, it really didn't feel much different than the other stunts she had pulled. I was genuinely concerned about the people who lost their homes, feeling terrible for them. I also didn't want my mom to be hurt but as drastic as it was, I knew this still wasn't her swan song. It was just *another* verse in her tragic story that seemed to never give her a redemptive chapter. I knew Becky expected me to want to talk about it, but I didn't have anything to say, so I changed the subject. "Are you at the office?"

"No, I'm at home today because we have our open

house tonight. I'm baking all kinds of cookies. You should see our kitchen. It's so overloaded, I had to set cooling racks on the wood floors in the hall."

"I can't believe you're baking. I would think your parents would cater it."

"They are bringing in the usual stuff from Martha's Bakery, but lately I want things to feel homey so I'm bringing a few trays of homemade stuff."

"So, in other words unless I want to gain ten pounds, I should not come home until you've cleared the building."

Becky giggled again, making me crack a tiny smile. "Actually," she said, her voice taking on an inquiring tone. "I decided I need to eat something decent before I dig into these treats, so I got stuff to make tacos. I wanted to see if you want to come home for lunch to eat with me?"

I lowered my eyes, knowing for a fact that Becky wasn't calling about tacos. She didn't want me to be alone right now because she thought I was sad. It was a sweet gesture and even though I had no appetite—and didn't even really like tacos—I knew Becky was reaching out to be a friend. Touched and truly grateful for her friendship, I didn't want to offend her by declining. "I guess I could take a break to come home for an hour. Do you need me to grab anything from the store?"

"No, I have way too much here. Just come as you are."

"Okay, I'll see you soon." I hung up the phone, and my attention was immediately detoured as I heard a shuffle behind me. I quickly turned my head to find Wally standing at my office door.

"Hey," he said. "Sorry, I was not trying to listen."

"It's fine." Waving him inside, I explained, "It was my roommate." I wiped the debris of that conversation from my face before I turned to him. "What's up?"

"I was going to get some lunch and I was wondering if you wanted me to grab you a salad or something?"

Triple blinking because I knew his timing was no accident, I was still taken aback by how yet another person was being thoughtful and trying to help me. "Normally, I'd say yes," I started, "but my roommate beat you to it. She's making tacos for me at our place . . ." Without deflecting my gaze, I had an idea and immediately offered, "Do you want to come with me?"

He shook his head, letting his overgrown mop of curls wag. "Nah, I can grab something by myself if you have plans."

"Actually, you should come," I insisted, feeling touched. "There should be plenty. Becky always cooks for a small army and it's only about a fifteen-minute walk, so it won't take that long."

"Do you want me to come?" I could tell his eyes were studying my face like he thought I was ready to crack into an ugly cry, so I made an extra effort to make sure I didn't look sad.

"Yes, I do," I said, then grabbed my purse from beside my desk, tucked my phone in the side pocket, and slung it over my shoulder as I stood. "Are you ready or do you need a sec? Because we should probably get going."

"You had me at tacos."

"And Becky seriously makes the best ones." I led the way out the door, and we quickly fell into step with each other on our way to my apartment, but I wanted to clear the air before things got too awkward, so I said, "I appreciate you being a friend, but I'm really not sad."

He gave a slight nod, like he wasn't buying it, but didn't comment any further. Wanting to convince him that I was perfectly capable of having a normal conversation, I asked, "Have you met my roommate before?"

He scrunched his lips to the side while he thought. "I don't think I've officially met her, but wasn't she the lady who showed up at the theatre looking for you?"

"Yep, that's her. We went to high school together. Well, actually we've known each other most of our lives because our moms have always been friends."

"Sort of like you and Fulton."

"No, not really the same. Eddie was my dad's friend. I knew Fulton, but I wasn't his friend." I chuckled, remembering some of the more embarrassing things Fulton had seen me do in my childhood. Then I shrugged. "But I guess it all worked out."

"I can't believe you guys got an apartment in this neighborhood," Wally observed as he motioned to the surrounding high-rises.

"That was all Becky. Her parents own a real estate company, and they sold this condo to an investment company last year. I'm not sure how they worked it out, but somehow her parents convinced them to rent it back to them while Becky is working as their office manager. I guess it's like a fringe benefit."

"Pretty nice fringe benefit."

"I'd say, and she barely charges me much for rent so I can seriously count my blessings on this deal."

"So, Becky wants to work in real estate too?"

"I'm not sure if she wants to or not, but I know she likes being close to her parents. She was sort of always the doted-on-princess. Especially with her dad, but both of her parents are super sweet." I pointed to the corner building that budded up next to Park Ave. "This is our building."

He raised an eyebrow. "Park Avenue?"

"No." I stopped him. "Technically, it's adjacent to it, but Becky's folks live in 'the' Park Avenue building." We passed through the front door together and I thought about how Wally and Becky actually had very similar backgrounds. Even though Wally didn't act like a rich kid, it was obvious his family was also very well-to-do. I led him to our apartment. "Are you ready for this?" I paused dramatically with my key in the front door, waiting to open it.

"I can literally smell the tacos through the front door."

Grinning, I pushed the door opened but he caught a glimpse of the room before I did. His jaw dropped, and he let out of knee-jerk laugh. I quickly followed his gaze. Becky had covered our tiny apartment with filled baking sheets. They lined the small kitchen counter and spread down the hallway—all the way to the bathroom. There were sugar cookies, dipped cookies, peanut butter blossom cookies, chocolate crinkle cookies, snowballs, shortbread cookies, and it looked like she was about halfway through a batch of monster cookies. "How on earth did you do this?" I marveled.

Her cheeks pinked when her eyes caught a hold of Wally, who I had failed to warn her was coming. "I couldn't decide what recipe to make, and I didn't want to run out."

"Where am I supposed to walk?" I dramatically moved to the side, trying to case along the wall.

"I can pick those up. I was in my flow and didn't want to stop." She grabbed a box from a pile on the couch. "I have boxes to fill so I can stack them, but I was waiting for them to cool as much as possible before I moved them."

"It's like a maze," Wally commented as he followed me inside, and before I forgot I motioned to him.

"I invited my boss for lunch. Have you met Wally?" I knew she knew all about him because I filled her in on my days at work and she had heard tons of Wally stories, but I still felt like an introduction was needed.

"No, not officially." Her eyes floated back to Wally, but her cheeks tinted again. I felt bad because I could tell she was embarrassed by her mess. "How do you do?" she asked Wally over the top of a cookie box.

"Good. And you?"

"I'm a little frazzled because I thought I had more time to clean up, but everything for lunch is ready. I just need to make room."

"I can help you," Wally said as he helped himself to two boxes from the stack and handed one to me. We both carefully shifted the cookies off the cookie sheets and into the boxes.

"I didn't know you were such a chef," I commented to Becky, trying to make her feel better.

"Me neither. I think I was hungry when I started."

"They all look great," Wally said.

"Fill a box for yourself," Becky offered. "What kind is your favorite?"

"I'm pretty boring, but I'm a classic sugar cookie guy."

"I have plenty of those. Oh, Abs!" Becky made an excited face, and her hand sprang forward pointing to a pan cooling on the table. "Did you see I made your favorites and they actually turned out?"

"I did see those, but I'm half expecting your old maid to come running up behind me, telling me to pick up my crumbs."

Becky's lips curled just enough to define her chin dimple. "She was crabby at you because you ate all her cookies, so she always had to make a double batch."

Sighing like I was being tossed into a fantasy. "Those were the days before I got serious about dance so I could eat a pan of cookies and not care." Then I reached for a cookie off her sheet and studied it before I pulled my lips back into a sly grin. "Good thing I'm not dancing anymore." With one bite, I was able to revive my taste buds of all the memories and I eagerly reached out again with my empty hand and selected a backup cookie.

Then we bellied up to the table and dug into the tacos, eating and talking lightheartedly—well, mostly Becky and I filled Wally in on our childhood memories. I started to wonder if he regretted coming to eat with us because he couldn't get a word in, but every time I checked, he was smiling and nodding pleasantly at our stories. Although he looked content to decipher our retellings, I was sure it was the tacos that were keeping him sane.

When we were done eating, we helped Becky load her cookie boxes into her ride-share and Wally and I headed back to the theatre. It was then that I realized I hadn't thought about my mom since we had walked over here. It was a small win for Becky and Wally—even though I knew I hadn't been sad.

"So . . ." Wally started. I knew he was going to bring up my mom and I didn't want to kill my good mood, so I cut him off."

"I'm fine, really. Yes, lunch helped to cheer me up, so your plan totally worked."

Wally's head tilted slightly, and his eyes steadied, looking surprised.

"Oh, I'm sorry. I thought for sure you would ask me if I was feeling better."

"Actually, I was going to ask you about Becky."

My brows bent down. Then in a flash that hit me like an alarm I realized he was asking me *about* Becky. I shot him a suspicious sideways glance and asked, "For real?"

He shrugged, maintaining a straight face that intrigued me because Wally hardly ever took anything seriously. "She's pretty cute and makes a mean taco."

"Becky is . . ." I hesitated, feeling my gut need a check because I didn't know how to answer this question. I trusted Wally enough that I would be friends with him, but I wasn't so sure how I felt about encouraging him to pursue anyone I cared about. I didn't know much about his dating life, but I did remember how he strung along his other girlfriend last year, which made me leery.

I chewed my lip, weighing his positive attributes. Wally was fun to be around, *but* I wasn't sure if he was Becky's type. Trying to remember who she liked in high school, I was stunned that I couldn't recall her dating much at all. She had always been gorgeous and never had a lack of interest, but she had also been extremely shy and quiet. I did remember one conversation we had after she turned down a date to our homecoming dance. She had seemed genuinely uninterested. And that was pretty much all I could remember about Becky's dating history. I missed a couple of years when I was living out of state, but she had never mentioned much about anyone. I could feel my face pinch further now because it did seem odd to me that I never noticed before that she had never had a boyfriend.

"You don't want me to say anything to her, do you?" Wally guessed from my silence.

"No . . ." I paused as I still didn't know what I thought. "Becky is . . ."

"Is available?"

"She doesn't have a boyfriend," I affirmed, "but—"

"But?"

I slowed so I could give him one of my looks of caution and in my best mom voice, I said, "She's not a girl to play around with." Then I found myself glaring at him, feeling oddly protective of her, but he never flinched.

"Okay," he said softly before asking, "Can you give me her number?"

I grimaced, imagining how weird things could get if Becky started dating my boss. I wasn't sure if Wally could be a gentleman and pursue a girl seriously and I was also sure Becky's lack of experience would leave her a little more vulnerable to being easily hurt by any weird games Wally might be up too. Then I reasoned they were both adults and it wasn't my business what either of them did, but regardless of how everything would turn out, Wally was still my boss—and I desperately needed my job—and Becky was still my roommate— and I desperately needed a roof over my head. "I'm not sure how she feels about it. Let me ask first."

"Okay. That's fine." We resumed a normal walking pace, but we didn't get very far before Wally said, "It's not a big deal if you don't want me to talk to her. I wasn't going to be a jerk or anything, but I understand if you're jealous."

"What?" My laugh came out in a sputter. "Hardly."

He was laughing too, and I barely heard my muffled phone ring through my purse. When I pulled it out, I saw it was Fulton calling. "Hey," I answered.

"Hey, where you at?"

"I'm walking back to work. Why?"

"Where were you?"

"Wally and I went to my house because Becky made lunch."

"Really?" Fulton's voice sounded disappointed. "Bummer. I'm at the theatre. I came into the city today to surprise you for lunch. I thought we'd have pork on a stick."

I smirked at how yet another person was trying to use food to cheer me up. "That is sweet of you, but I'm stuffed."

"Well, how far are you?"

"Maybe another ten minutes."

"That's too bad because I've actually been waiting here for over a half hour thinking you'd come back, but if you already ate, I might head back so I can catch this hour's train. I have a meeting with my advisor at two."

Feeling instantly bummed that I wasn't going to see him—even though I hadn't been expecting to be able to see him today—I didn't want to make him feel bad, so I said, "That's cool. Maybe later this week we can eat pork on sticks?"

"For sure. I'll call you after my meeting."

"Sounds good." I hung up my phone and caught a glimpse of Wally giving me a funny look.

"What?"

"I was wondering what Fulton will do when he finds out you're jealous that I think Becky's cute."

"Stop!" I elbowed him again.

He laughed, giving me his daring grin. "Give me her number then."

I glared at him, lifting up my mom finger. "If I give you her number, then you'll stop this ridiculous assumption that I'm jealous before it gets out of hand?"

"Yes," he said with conviction.

I flashed my eyes heavenward, then I opened my contacts on my phone, searched for her number, and then forwarded it in a text message to him. I was half annoyed, but the bigger half of me was slightly scared to death.

Wally's lips broadened up into a wide curve when he looked back over at me. I was ready for him to make a joke that would prick at my nerves more, but instead, his eyes lowered, sending off an air of sweetness, but I still wasn't convinced when he said, "I'm not going to be a jerk."

"You better not." I wanted to grin back, but I couldn't. Wally was my friend, but more importantly, he was my boss. He was in all the ways a "good guy" but somehow when I thought about him wanting to be with Becky, good wasn't a descriptive word I could use anymore. I had a bad feeling about this.

Chapter Three

Upon returning to the theatre with a bloated taco belly, I rushed to my office prepared to send Becky an apology warning text about Wally having her number. I was pressing the send button when Wally tapped on my open door. My eyes landed on a silver gift bag that hung loosely from his fingers. Before I could ask, he explained, "This was sitting on the ticket box window with a note that it's for you."

Confused, I held out my hand to retrieve the bag and peeked at the sticky note attached, quickly identifying Fulton's handwriting. My heart swelled instantly, and I felt a little pitter-patter thumb against my rib cage as I peered into the sack to see a bottomless pile of Hersey Kisses. "This is so sweet," I said out loud, but I was thoroughly perplexed as to what the occasion was, and I hoped it wasn't another way to feed away my mom issues. Then I noticed a little blue corner of a card peeking out of the pile and I reached my thumb and pointer finger inside and pulled it out. Without hesitation, I ripped open the envelope and read it.

Can you please think about coming home with me to Montana? – Fulton.

I would be lying if I said my breath didn't get caught in my chest. One part of me marveled at the way Fulton understood me and I appreciated his gentle, adorable way he approached these issues. However, the bigger part of me had no intentions of ever going back to Montana. Add in the recent passing of my dad, I just wasn't ready to be around other people's happy families when I couldn't be with my own.

"Trouble in paradise?" Wally's voice startled me out of my trance as I had forgotten he was still standing in my doorway.

I scratched the front of my neck and lowered the card back into the bag. "Nah, he's just being sweet Fulton."

His dark eyes remained expressionless when he said in a soft voice, "You're lucky you have him."

"I am," I said, whole-heartily believing my words.

I thought we'd be done talking since we had just got back from our lunch break, but Wally surprised me by taking the conversation a little deeper. "I remember watching you last year as you were chasing after him and wondering if you would ever work your issues out, but I have to say that since you guys have gotten together, I've seen a lot of positive changes from both of you. I'm sort of envious."

"Envious?" I repeated, waiting for him to give me the punchline.

"Yeah, I see how you support each other, and I think it's nice. I wish I had that."

I knew the look I gave him was more on the skeptic than on the empathic side. I still had a thread of suspicion that ran through my brain waves when I thought about Wally in a relationship, and now I was more on edge because I knew he still had Becky's number burning a hole in his pocket. "Did you text Becky yet?"

His brows sprang up, like he had forgotten, so then I mentally kicked myself for reminding him. I expected his mischievous grin, but instead, he lowered his eyes again. "I didn't. I wanted to but then I got nervous."

"What?" my disbelieving voice sprang out. "You're not nervous."

"I sort of am."

I was about to tease him, but I could see him shuffle his feet like he did when he was getting started with a new joke on stage. In the moment it made him appear lightly innocent, which I knew he clearly wasn't, so I broke out laughing.

"It's not funny," he retorted.

"Sorry." I covered my mouth. "I've never seen you act shy."

"I don't know why I'm acting like this either. I was fine talking to her at your place, but then once you gave me her number, it got really different."

I had a brief wave of relief wash over me, thinking that Wally might chicken out and leave all the things to Becky unsaid, but that relief was short-lived because he stated, "I'm going to text her tonight when I'm not distracted."

I think he expected me to give him a pep talk, but I couldn't. My heart wrenched for all the heartache Wally was going to cause Becky. Vowing to sternly warn her about Wally as soon as I got home, I looked back at him, fighting to find a way to nonchalantly talk him out of texting her but all I could come up with was an uneasy grin and tiny words. "If it's meant to be. . ." Then I awkwardly shrugged my shoulder because the last thing I wanted to do was encourage him. Thankfully a low vibrating sound from my phone interrupted us. My eyes skirted to see it was Fulton again, and I confirmed it to Wally. "It's him."

"I'll give you some privacy." He backed out of my doorway, and I smiled wistfully as I answered the phone, both relieved to be done with *that* conversation and excited to talk to Fulton. "Hey," I answered.

"Hey." Fulton's tone was cool and easy.

"How was your meeting?"

"It went well. We went over my official list of schools I'm applying for, and he had a letter of recommendation that he had ready for me to add to my packets, so I feel good."

"Schools?" I asked, confused. "I thought you said you wanted to go to Cornell."

"Oh, I definitely do, but I don't get to pick. I have to be selected, so it's always good to apply to tons of schools and even then, some more safety schools."

"That makes sense." I felt at ease knowing he was

the smartest person I knew, so if he didn't get into his top choice of schools, then no one would.

"So . . ." His voice fished.

"So . . ." I shyly echoed, knowing where he was taking this conversation.

"Did you find something in your office?"

"I did. Well, no, Wally found it and gave it to me."

"And?"

"And . . ."

"And my mom is having Christmas next weekend since I wasn't able to get a flight over the holiday. I checked and they have a couple of seats left at a great rate. I would love to have you come with me."

I drank in a deep breath and innocently asked, "Did Christmas come again this year?"

He lightly chuckled and I expected him to continue with this path but sweet Fulton—who knew my heart too well—pivoted. "Do you have any chocolate left?"

"I actually haven't touched them. I had way too many cookies at lunch and for a girl who is now selling a dance clothing line, I need to be eating better—"

"Please," he interrupted, "you always look great."

"Thank you." I accepted his compliment. Even though I knew he was supposed to say those things because he was my boyfriend, a warm rush of dopamine still found its way to fill my heart.

"So, I'll see you tomorrow for pork on a stick?"

"Deal. See you tomorrow."

"I can't wait."

"Bye," I said a little flatly because I had honestly been glad to have Christmas over this year. It was the first year without my dad, and I had been happy to sit at home by myself and binge-watch ballets. I knew Fulton was being insanely sweet about this and I didn't want to let him down, but the thought of going to Montana—now without my dad—made me physically ill.

Chapter Four

The next day, promptly at noon, Fulton handed me my beloved pork on a stick, and I inhaled the garlicy goodness while we headed to our usual spot of cement next to the building. We sat side by side while we people watched and chowed. "You're a cheap date," Fulton said in between bites. He had an extra stick of pork today because he had brought along a shelter dog who was extremely well mannered, staying right on Fulton's heel while he waited to be offered his pork.

"I think it's because we spent all that time in the wilderness and now it feels like a wonder to me that you can get cooked pork on a random street corner."

"It doesn't hurt that it's delicious too." Fulton pulled the pork off in pieces and fed his new friend, who slurped it up and swallowed it in one bite.

"That too." I chewed for a moment then motioned to the dog. "What's his story?"

"I was cleaning out kennels and he took a liking to me, and he looked like he needed some exercise. Then I figured since I have the rest of the afternoon free, I can easily drop him off on my way to night class."

"He's sort of cute in that mangy sort of way."

"It's rustic." Fulton laughed and then added, "I should give him a bath before I leave, but there is always so much work to do at the shelter that it's overwhelming."

My eyes skirted to the side to get a direct hit on his when I asked, "Speaking of the shelter, did you line up my cats?"

He lowered his eye into a wink that I think was supposed to have been flirty, but it came out way too overplayed, especially when he added the slow-motion nod and said, "I'm on it."

I couldn't help but laugh and then playfully leaned my head on his shoulder, wrapped my arm around his chest, and squeezed. "You're the best. Thanks!"

"You bet."

"I would kiss you right now, but I just woofed down like fourteen cloves of garlic."

"I'm not a vampire, so I can totally handle it."

I gritted my teeth playfully. "Are you sure about that?"

"I mean, sometimes at night I black out and wake up in random trees hanging upside down, but I think that's normal, right?"

"Totally. Happens to me all the time." I chuckled under my breath, before I let my eyes spring open wider. "So, I have gossip, I guess."

Fulton's brows bent down. "You actually talk to people to gossip about?"

"I'm not that antisocial."

"I'm not saying I've been super social lately either because I've been studying all the time, but I think we are both anti-social to a fault."

"You are probably right, but nevertheless I do have gossip."

"Okay." Fulton's lips quivered like he was trying to keep a straight face, but it was obvious he expected my gossip to be ridiculous.

"So, um, Wally took Becky out on a date last night."

He blinked a few extra times before settling on an easy one-word question. "How?"

"I'm guessing they walked."

"No, not like how they went out, but how did that happen?"

"It was my stupid fault. I invited Wally over for lunch because he invited me first. He thought I was sad about my mom. Then Becky made amazing tacos. It was apparently like a trap."

Fulton chuckled lightly. "How do you think it went?"

"I don't know. Becky was gone when I got up this morning, but Wally came into work whistling and that was new."

"Whistling? Why would that have anything to do with Becky?"

"I'm not saying it does, but I didn't even know he could whistle and this morning it was so loud I wanted to scream at him to shut up, but I also didn't want to get fired."

"Well, cool." Fulton took a moment to push his bottom lip out. "That might be good for them."

I scrunched my nose, wondering why he would say something so positive. "Good for them?"

"Yeah, I mean, think about it. If it works out, we can all group date. That would be a blast and I'd be happy for them."

I was speechless that he wasn't horrified by the idea of Wally dating Becky the way I was. He must have picked up on my uneasiness and asked, "You aren't happy for them?"

"No." I took a moment to adjust my grimace. "I know Wally's your friend and he is my friend, but I don't trust him with her."

"Why not?"

"Why would I?"

Fulton lowered his voice defensibly. "He's been really good to you. For one, he created a job for you, and I think it would be nice to see him happy with someone."

"It's weird, though, because they just met and now they are dating already."

"One date doesn't mean they are dating."

"I guess we don't see it the same way . . ." I let my voice trail off because I was done talking about how weird I was feeling over the ordeal, especially when it was clear we were on different pages. I let my eyes drift back to the dog and noticed a bundle tied around his neck that I pointed to and asked, "What's this?"

"That" –Fulton flashed his flirty boy grin at me— "is a present that Chester brought for you."

"What?" My brows pulled up when I realized Fulton had brought the dog to use as a prop.

He motioned to the bundle. "Go ahead and take it."

I held my hand out for Chester to smell me; my lips curled when his damp nose sniffed over the top of my hand. "Here, boy, can I have my present?" He licked my hand and then let me easily untie the pouch from his collar. "What did you get me?" I asked Fulton while I unwrapped the little bundle.

"They aren't from me," Fulton maintained. "Chester wanted you to have them."

Fuzzy red and white stripes appeared, and I quickly identified them to be a pair of socks. My heart fluttered as it was incredibly cute to use the dog and all, and I totally knew what Fulton was up to. I held them up. "So my feet don't get cold when I'm in Montana?"

"I got us matching pairs so we can be *that* cheesy couple."

Seriously, my heart totally melted like chocolate on a hot marshmallow for all his efforts. "Well, at least it wasn't the full jammies."

"Just wait." He held up a finger, wagging it at me playfully. "I might have that covered."

Then my eyes diverted from his while I fidgeted with the socks. "I appreciate the gift but—"

"They are one-size fits most. They will totally fit you even after you eat all the chocolate I bought you."

I knew Fulton had cut me off so I couldn't refuse him, and I didn't want to resist the gift, but I did have a budding seed of anxiety in my gut now. Okay, it was more than a seed. I'd call it more like a planet-sized ball of anxiety because I was still torn wide-open over the loss of my dad. I waited until I had a deep exhale to let my eyes rise to meet his, but he winked right when I latched, making my heart wrench even more. "You aren't going to let me say no, are you?"

He put his arm around my shoulder, pulling me into a side hug. "I know you want to stay home and be sad, but I think it would do you some good to come back with me and get away for a while." When I didn't reply, he added, "Plus, Chester thinks you will look adorable in those socks, and I sort of think he's right."

I sighed, holding my eyes in communion with his. "Well, if Chester thinks so . . ."

The grin that spread on Fulton's face spoke right to my heart, and I knew it was worth it so I could make him happy. He was easily the best thing to happen to me —ever. For that, I was willing to suffer through this trip, especially since I knew it would only be a few days.

Chapter Five

Later that night, I worked late, trying to get the fittings on my dancers completed. Once I'd finished with the last girl's measurements, I retreated to my office, noticing the room had looked like it had been burglarized. I wasn't messy, but I wasn't an overly organized person either. Something about the events of the last few days had left me in a constant state of on edge and apparently that caused me to scatter things all over like a toddler who didn't understand things had a proper place.

Vowing to be more careful with Nana's antiques, I wiped off her dressing table and tried to buff out a small scratch on the corner. I didn't remember having anything sharp on the table, but judging from the look of it, it could have happened from my keys or anything of that manner. My efforts were unsuccessful in the moment, and it was late, so I decided it would have to do for now. Then I reached under my desk lamp and shut it off and flipped the switch on the overhead light, leaving only the glow of a small plug-in night light I had added when I had slept here. I kept it because I loved the ambiance it created of being able to be in this grand dressing room when it was illuminated with an amber glow. Feeling serene and almost frozen in time, I could forget that outside the room, the world was still moving to a tempo too fast for me. I grabbed my purse and my reusable coffee mug just as I heard Wally's measured footsteps on the old squeaky back-stage wood. I turned to greet him, and he met my hello by saying, "I was locking up and saw your light still on."

"This was the only time I could do Bre's fitting because she had late dance classes, but I got all the girls done, so my head is in a better place."

"Good." He jingled his keys in his hands. "It's late. I can walk you part-way if you want."

"I'll be fine." I grabbed my phone from Nana's table and was about to drop it into my bag when it lit up, signaling a call. I assumed it was Fulton, but a second glance made me realize the number was out of state. "Just a second," I told Wally as I positioned my phone to answer it. "Hello."

I didn't know the voice on the other line, but I didn't need to. He said four words that immediately put my stomach into a knot. I thanked him for his call, then hung up the phone, quickly stowing it into my bag, trying to act like it was a wrong number. Using my best avoidance maneuver, I sidestepped to try to exit my office and called to Wally over my shoulder as casually as I could, "Are you coming?"

But Wally wasn't leaving, and he deadpanned right on me. "Abs, you're shaking."

"It might be chilly down here. That reminds me to grab my trench coat." With a fluid motion, I reached behind the open door and grabbed the heavy coat I had stowed on the hook. Then I slipped it on and tied the belt all while doing my best to look breezy and set out to leave again, but Wally stood blocking my way out of my office.

"Who was that?" he asked. His eyes seemed to call mine to his, but I dug deep to avoid them.

Put off by his invasiveness, I winced. "Nobody really."

He looked at his watch and then slowly looked back at me. "Well, it's almost nine and so it's past general courtesy call times. The color drained from your face as soon as you talked to that person. It's a little concerning for me to see you like this. Seriously, I'm thinking somebody has to have died."

"Hardly." I breathed out sarcastically, but my joke didn't let me off the hook with Wally because his eyes stayed steady on mine.

"Is everything okay?" he asked again. His words were careful like he was asking permission to talk.

"It's fine. Notta big deal." I tried again to brush his concern away, but I could see he wasn't satisfied with my answer and so without planning to, I blurted out, "They found my mom." The word mom seemed to echo in the room like we were in an abandoned building, but each

43

echo acted like a dagger digging into my heart. I hadn't missed her—obviously. I had barely even thought about her. I mean, I was used to her being gone. I certainly wasn't worried about her because that would have been silly. Of course, I hadn't been sad, so I wasn't sure why the news of her safety would bring me into such a state of emotion, but my arm suddenly got too weak to hold my overstuffed bag and I had to let my purse drop to the floor as I burst into tears.

It was awkward to cry in front of Wally—but yet oddly fitting because it did seem that over the last couple of years, Wally had been the one who had always sneakily been here for me. He was never my first choice for a confidant but somehow, he had managed to always be in my space when I melted down. Then I realized that maybe it was best that he had been the one here. Becky would have flooded me with questions, out of concern, of course. Even Fulton would have made a big deal about my emotional outburst, feeling like he had the responsibility to cheer me up. However, Wally just stood there, not unsympathetic in any way, but I think he was probably feeling helpless to do anything other than to just be.

When I was able to find my composure, I blew my nose a few times in a tissue and then tucked a handful of spare tissues safely into my coat pocket—just in case. Then I wiped the last of the dampness from my cheek with the back of my hand, noting the tears had a cooling effect that helped to balance my mood again and I was feeling grounded by the time I was finally able to meet his eyes again and said, "Sorry."

"It's okay. It's a lot to process."

He never asked again if he could walk me home, but he did. We didn't talk. I was too in my head, thinking about my mom and he again, was probably too stunned to know what to say, but it was sort of nice to have him there. When we got to my building, I said goodnight and turned to go inside, but not before I watched him steal a glimpse at our living room window that overlooked the street. His action was sort of displaced and it made me wonder if he had hoped to actually steal a look at Becky. As I walked up the stairs to our place, I was suddenly reminded of their date last night. If it bothered me before, now I sort of welcomed a new distraction for my brain and I quick-ened my steps, hoping to catch Becky awake before bed.

I took the stairs two at a time, until I reached the third floor and quietly let myself into our corner unit. "I'm home," I called out softly after I latched the door. I could see Becky's light on under her bedroom door, so I knew she was awake, but she didn't respond to my greet-ing. I hung up my coat and dropped my bag on the floor, then crossed over to her room where I rested my ear next to the door. The room was silent. I tapped lightly, careful not to wake her if she had been sleeping. "Bec," I whispered.

"Yeah," she called back. "It's open."

When I pushed the door and entered her room, I found her curled up in bed in her white fuzzy robe and matching slippers. Her fiery red hair was knotted on top of her head and she totally looked like she belonged in a luxury spa. Her phone rested next to her and still glowed like she had just used it.

"Hey," she greeted me softly.

Her voice was too tender, giving away her secret, and I immediately busted her. "Wally texted you about my mom?"

She scrunched her nose like she wasn't sure what to say. "He texted telling me he had walked you home and I asked if there was something wrong."

I gave her a weird, suspicious look like I wasn't sure who she was anymore. "So now you guys are texting?"

She let out an airy laugh, but her face lit up. "I guess."

I didn't want to talk about my mom. I also didn't want to talk about Wally either, but that was the better of the two horrible conversations. Plus, I could tell Becky had this weird glow thing going on with her cheeks that I had never seen before, and I had to imagine that she was dying inside to tell someone what was making her feel like that. So, I did my best to try not to vomit when I sat next to her on her bed. "How was your date with Wally?"

It was evident that she was holding back her smile to appease the gloomy mood I was in. However, she did let a reserved smile escape before she said, "It was . . . nice."

"Nice?" Trying to hide my sarcasm, I pretended to be genuinely interested.

"Yeah, we didn't do anything, really. We went for a drink and then ended up roaming around the city, walking and talking." She shrugged but not in a bewildered sort of way, more like in a feeling shy way. "He's so easy to talk to," she added, and I could tell she was scared to tell me more and that made me sad. I didn't want to be a friend who ruined her glow. I wanted to be the girlfriend she could tell anything and everything to.

So instead of bemoaning how dumb she was for dating Wally, I admitted, "He is easy to talk to." That was honestly one of the truest things about Wally. He was one of those rare people I'd been able to let my guard down with because I knew that he would never act better than me.

She picked up on my comment and gushed, "It was amazing how much we had to talk about. We literally couldn't stop talking and I felt so comfortable telling him all about my childhood and just . . . everything."

"He is one of the least judgmental people I know."

"And he is so funny too"—her voice quickened as she went on—"he wants me to come see his show on Saturday. He said I should ask you to come with me, so I don't have to sit alone, but he said you are more than likely sick of seeing his face. I said I could convince you to come with me, though." Then she paused and smiled at me sweetly.

"Well, yeah. I practically live there but Saturday is my day off. I usually try to spend it with Fulton, but I can bring him with too. We can make a night of it," I offered, trying to match her enthusiasm.

"That would be so fun!" she exclaimed with so much excitement I was overwhelmed. It was like I could see the wheels of her brain churn as they switched gears and she immediately asked me in a lower voice of concern, "What am I going to wear? Will you help me?"

I wanted to groan at the thought of her wanting to impress Wally, but it was cute to see her so flustered over a guy because I had never seen her like that. Even though I still didn't know what to think about Wally and wondered if he was playing games, I desperately hoped he was sincere in his efforts with her because in the moment, Becky was happy and for that, I was happy too. I was happy to see her happy and even more grateful she had forgotten to ask about my mom.

Chapter Six

"Look at us, going out on a non-pork related date tonight?" Fulton proclaimed as soon as he caught a glimpse of Becky and me approaching the theatre together the following Saturday night.

"Don't trash talk our pork-on-a-stick dates," I teasingly warned him as I joined him by his side and latched my arm into his.

"I'm not." He held his palms up like he had been caught. "We don't usually go out in public, especially on a Saturday night." When I scanned his face, I could tell he had recently shaved—which frankly was sort of a rare thing these days and then I did a double take, noting another rarity—a blue collared shirt. I grinned approvingly as it was definitely nice to see him wearing something other than his collegian sweatshirts.

"Yeah, we might need to make more of an effort to

be social," I said, knowing too well that it had been a long while since I had entered the theatre like this—linked in hand with Fulton. It didn't take long before the anticipation of the night sent a pleasant thrill of goose bumps up my spine and I smiled affectionately at my sweet boyfriend.

Then I turned toward Becky as we passed the row seating and explained, "It's sort of our custom to always sit at the front table. Wally calls it VIP seating, but it's more like the seats you sit on if you want to be picked on."

Becky listened as she followed me down the aisle and took a seat across from Fulton and me. Then it was only a short moment more and the hall lights dimmed. The stage lights got brighter, hushing the audience. Fulton squeezed my hand, and I glanced at him. His eyes swept over, motioning for me to look at Becky where I could see in her profile eagerness so strong you'd have thought Wally was a celebrity. But he wasn't. He was just a boy Becky had met last week. I wouldn't have believed it if I hadn't seen the events unfold for myself, but it was becoming more evident that she was developing a monster crush on him, and I hoped for her sake that he was crushing too.

When the show was over, Becky practically flew over to Wally and they quickly made plans to go for a late-night dinner. I wasn't hungry so I declined and since I didn't have any desire to spend extra time at the theatre on my night off, we split up when Fulton offered to walk me home. Fulton and I chatted on the way to my house, mostly about Wally's current skit. It wasn't my favorite, but it wasn't bad. Fulton thought it would have been better if he'd had more impressions.

"I do think it was nice for us to get a little gussied up and go out," I admitted, stealing one more look at how handsome he looked. "I never realized how boring we are."

"Not boring," Fulton defended. "Just busy. I think too, since you work in entertainment, it sort of takes the pleasure out of attending those events, so when you're not working, you don't really want to go to a movie or anything like that where there are tons of people."

"That's exactly it." I agreed and my apartment building was now in view, so I shot a sideways look at him and offered, "Do you want to come upstairs? It's still early."

"Sure, I can come up for a bit," he agreed, following me inside, but I noticed he had gotten strangely quiet right after that, so I tried to fill in the silence with random thoughts.

"I think Becky prolly still has at least four dozen cookies in our freezer that someone other than me needs to eat, so I'm going to pull those out for you."

"I think I'd need my stretchy pants for that," Fulton joked while he touched his stomach. "Remember I actually wore dress pants tonight."

"Bummer," I said, pulling my baby doll dress forward to show how far it stretched. "Because I have lots of room in my stomach." He laughed lightly at my joke, but I could hear something off about his tone, like it was a little forced and maybe even distracted. So when I let us into my apartment, I kept one eye on him when I took the time to hang up our coats and then offered, "I haven't been home much, so I'm not sure what I have on hand, but do you want something to drink?" I walked over to the fridge and peered inside, randomly calling out the contents that looked nontoxic: water, energy drinks, some sort of tea thing with floaties on top that Becky liked. "Oh and I do have what looks like half a bottle of sparkling wine, circa last weekend from when Becky's parents were here for dinner."

"Water is fine," he called from where he took a seat on the couch, resting his feet on our tiny ottoman slash coffee table.

I grabbed two waters and a bag of frozen cookies from the freezer and headed over to the couch. "I wasn't kidding about the cookies." I held up the bag but then my eyes got a glimpse of something he was holding out for me to see—a piece of paper that was tri-folded like a letter. Not only was it a letter, but my heart instantly told me *this* was the distraction I had heard in his laugh when I reached for it. "What's this?"

"I got it earlier today but wanted to wait until we were alone to show it to you."

He watched me opened, and I felt my brows pull in confusion when I saw the header was from a college in Florida, but I read on and determined it was an acceptance letter for a veterinary program. There was also a large stipend and scholarship offer included in the offer. When I finished reading it, I folded it and handed it back to him, saying, "I don't get it. Why would a college in Florida accept you?"

I waited for him to talk, but when he didn't, I raised my eyes to meet his and froze, seeing that his eyes had widened considerably, looking completely vulnerable. Then his words came out slow and thoughtful, "So, this is a super long story that I never had the guts to tell you."

My throat got a little itchy from his vague introduction and I felt the need to clear it before I asked, "What do you mean?"

"Do you remember that one year at Christmas when your dad offered to make some calls to get me an internship?"

"Vaguely."

"Well, he ended up calling this one guy named, Rich, who said he didn't think they were hiring interns for the summer because he was planning to get a new job teaching for a university. The guy confessed that he was nervous, though, because although he had been practicing as a vet for decades, he wasn't much of a public speaker, and in order to get past the university hiring process, he needed to give a formal presentation." He hesitated, took a breath, then continued, "So, your dad did what your dad does and offered to help this dude out by making him this elaborate presentation complete with sound effects and music. Your dad said he spend like forty hours on this presentation, and it wowed everyone so much he got the job."

"I believe it." A pressure from behind my eyes appeared, reminding me how much I missed my dad, but I fought it off by blinking and micro-focusing on Fulton's lips moving, which wasn't hard to do because I loved his lips.

"So, your dad of course refused monetary payment, insisting instead that Rich had to remember me when the time came for me to apply to vet school. The guy agreed and took my name."

"That's cool."

"That's not all." His hand opened in a gesture toward me. "Do you remember that time I went to visit your dad in Virginia, right before he died?"

"Yes." My voice was way too soft, and I barely heard it, but I wasn't going to repeat myself, so I waited.

"I went there for a few reasons. One was, I knew he was sick, and I wanted to say goodbye. However, he had also told me he had something to talk to me about. When I got there, he asked me about vet school, and that's when he explained all this to me about how he had done this presentation and made me promise that I would apply to this school. This school wasn't ever on my radar as anywhere I'd go, but your dad insisted that I apply so I agreed. I never forgot about that conversation, or my promise.

Well, out of the blue about a month ago, I got an email from this guy. He said they had an opening for a teaching assistantship, and he wanted to recommend me for it and then he asked if I could send in my packet early. I sort of thought it was surreal, but I thought why not—and I did promise your dad." He pointed to the letter. "I have no idea how your dad closed this deal, but it had to be him. If you read the letter—not only am I admitted into the program—I'm offered a teaching stipend, on top of their biggest scholarships. I did the math, and I would probably come out money ahead."

My brows knitted together because I hadn't known any of this stuff about my dad. It felt like a strange gift that didn't make any sense because he had known Fulton wanted to go to a vet school on Long Island. I wasn't really sure why Fulton had bothered to do the math, but I reckoned that it felt good to be accepted into any program even if it wasn't the one you wanted to attend, so I forced my lips to turn upward. "Well, of course they want you to come to their school. You're the best vet student there is."

"Not the best, but I work hard," he said with modest undertones.

"I can totally believe my dad did that." I leaned back on the couch and grabbed a blanket that had been hanging over the back, pulling it to cover us both up into a comfortable snuggle. "I have a feeling you have a lot more of those letters coming, so I'm excited to see how these colleges fight for you."

Fulton took the edge of the blanket I had offered him, pulling it over his lap, at the same time wrapping his arm around the back of my shoulders. "I don't think they'll be fighting, but it feels good to see I'm off to a good start." Then he dug back into his back pocket, producing another piece of paper and held it out to me. "This one is for you."

"Now what?" I took the paper, unfolding it. "Is it a bill?" I joked, completely clueless about what another piece of paper would say, but my joke fell flat when I saw it was an airplane itinerary to Montana with my name on it.

"Don't frown," he warned.

"I'm not frowning. I was caught off guard." I flashed the ticket back at him. "You didn't have to get a ticket for me. I would have paid for it."

"I wanted to get it as a gift, and I had to make sure you got on the right plane." His perfect teeth peeked out from his teasing smile.

"Thank you for the gift . . ."

"You're welcome." A pleased grin stamped on his lips, but it only lasted a moment before he let it slip away. "So . . ." Fulton's tonal change warned of a shift of subject. I looked back at him, sort of feeling like I knew what he was going to bring up. With a look of endearment, he pushed back a stray hair that had fallen out of my ponytail and said, "You seem really distant lately."

I blinked, sending out a warning for him. *Don't bring up my mom.* I knew he knew they had found my mom, but I never told him. That was one of those special privileges I enjoyed from having Wally intercept that meltdown. I was sure it seemed weird to Fulton that I never directly told him, but Fulton was used to my weirdness, and he also never held it against me. "I don't want to talk about it." Tucking my bottom lip in, I turned away.

"What *it* are you referring to?"

"My mom, of course," I defended, a little shocked he made me confirm it out loud.

"Really? It seems like you're more bothered by Becky and Wally."

My head jerked back. "What?"

"Yeah." His head bobbed. "You went off the other day about it and I didn't say anything, but I could tell by the way you looked at the two of them together tonight that you are uneasy about something."

I wished I could deny it, claiming that wasn't a true accusation, but he was dead-on. I was uneasy. And worse, the more I tried to find the words to explain my frustration, I didn't know what I was upset about. Becky was my friend. Wally was my friend. I was happy for my friends. They seemed happy. On paper, it seemed perfect, but I was bothered. I gave a curt shrug. "Maybe you are right, but I don't know why I'm bothered by it."

"Do you not think Wally is good enough for Becky?"

"No, it's not that." I stared off, while I tried to analyze what my indecisive mind was trying to tell me. "It feels weird since they literally just met, and they are so open to trusting one another. I think I'm more scared than Becky is that she might get hurt."

Fulton slowly nodded. "That totally makes sense that that's what's bothering you. I can't believe I didn't pin it down for myself."

"What makes sense?"

"You have trust issues. Of course you think she's going to get hurt because you have a hard time thinking anything can ever end in a happy ending."

"That's not true."

His eyebrow perked. "Says the girl who still is incapable of using the L word."

I shuddered, feeling like he was exposing one of my inadequacies. "That's not fair."

"I'm not bringing it up to pick on you. I understand where you are coming from and I respect those things are different for you, but not everyone has a giant wall around their heart."

His facial expression was indifferent. I knew he wasn't trying to provoke a fight, nor was he judging me. He had never complained that I was a snail when it came to saying the L word, but I sometimes wondered if maybe it did bother him. Part of me was thinking that he wouldn't have brought it up if it didn't annoy him. After a quiet moment, I asked, "You do know how I feel about you, right?"

"I do." His eyes latched on mine, and I felt a shiver run down my spine from the pause he held. "That's why I don't ever bring it up."

"It's a hard word for me to say and I also think a person can have feelings without having to talk about them and define them."

"They can . . . but most therapists will probably tell you it's healthiest to define your feelings and to also express them." His words were more matter-of-fact than hinting at personal offense.

"Maybe I need to work on that then," I admitted more to myself than to him as this conversation was bumming me out because Fulton meant everything to me. I knew I had issues with expressing feelings especially when it came to the L word, but I felt I had a just reason. I had never really used that word before. I spent my childhood thinking I had to do something to get my mom to feel that way, and when all my attempts to make her heart shine for me always fell flat, I was left feeling unworthy of hearing that word and also self-conscious about speaking it. Now, as an adult, when I did try to use it, it brought up a lot of stuff from my childhood, and I didn't want that baggage in my relationship with Fulton. But I knew he was right, so I put my hand on his knee and said, "I'm going to work on it."

"You're working on what?"

I flashed a big L that I made with my hand using my thumb and forefinger. "I'm going to work on feeling good when I say this word."

Eyeing my big L, a slow grin seeped onto his face like he thought I was ridiculous. Then he held up his hand to match my big L. "So this is where we are starting. With a hand signal L."

"It's a start."

"It's like an E.T. version of affection." He chuckled, holding the new hand signal up like he was trying to communicate with aliens.

I took a nearby throw pillow and smacked it over his alien sign language. "Stop it. Now I feel dumb."

He kept laughing as he pulled the pillow out of my hand and tucked it under his arm for safety. "Sorry, it's sort of cute."

I rubbed one eye like I knew I was losing my mind; I knew it was dumb, that I could just say it but when I tried to bring the words to my lips, they just wouldn't come. So, I firmly replied, "I'm going to get better. I just need practice."

"Deal." Then with a sarcastic smirk on his face he held out his big L like he was wanting a fist bump.

I chuckled at how this conversation had turned into

something so total nonsense and tapped his L with mine. "You're a dork.".

"We are dorks together."

"Yes, we are," I agreed, not wanting it any other way.

Chapter Seven

"Phew." I blew out the last of my breath while dropping my cardboard box—stuffed with the newest delivery of costumes—onto the middle of the stage. When I straightened back up, I let one hand linger on my side, massaging where it had strained. "That was heavier than I thought," I huffed.

Wally chuckled at me from where he hunched over a notebook, working on his own project of mapping out the new stage set. His eyes flicked from my television-sized box back to me. "What are you even doing here this late?"

"I'm waiting on Bre again. Her costumes didn't look right, so I wanted to do another fitting before we start dress rehearsals this week."

Wally's head bobbed in acknowledgment. "Well, I appreciate all your hard work. It's been amazing to be able to hand this over to someone who takes it so seriously."

A trickle of pride bubbled up into my chest and I said, "You're welcome." I enjoy the work here and most of the time it doesn't feel like work as much as it feels like any other creative project I would do."

His lips parted, then he let his eyes hover over mine. "So, are you doing okay with *everything*?"

I knew by the sympathetic expression on his face, he wasn't asking about my work anymore. I avoided the urge to bite back with a sarcastic comment, lowering my eyes while I collected my thoughts into words I thought would satisfy his friendly curiosity while also laminating the topic from further probing. "I'm going to visit her right after I get back from Montana. I don't have time to fit it in before we leave in two days."

"That'll be nice for her to see you," he said softly.

"I doubt it," I muttered under my breath.

I thought my snide comment would tip him off to the fact that I was forlorn about the whole situation, and I didn't want to talk about her. But he found a way to eye trap me and I felt exposed, like I was being busted for something illegal, and my cheeks warmed. "What?" I asked innocently.

He angled his head toward me, but he stayed silent while maintaining his eye lock.

A weird vibe was brewing. Maybe it was from my extreme exhaustion, but I got instantly perturbed that he would even linger on this topic about my mom when he came from a perfect family. "You're judging me, aren't you?" I accused flatly.

"No," he said without flinching. "I'm definitely not one in any position to judge."

"Then what is it?" I asked, feeling myself subconsciously tuck a defensive hand on my hip while I squared my body.

He didn't match my aggression, though. Instead, he relaxed, stretching backward, bracing himself with his hand. "I've actually been thinking about you a lot. And your mom."

I felt my throat restrict like it was being wrung out like a wet rag. "Oh," was all I could supply.

"And your relationship with her."

I could feel his eyes survey my face, but I held my expression steady. Now the rag wringing sensation was moving down into my chest and I was pretty confident if this conversation didn't end shortly, I would suffocate. My feet propelled me forward, and I swiftly dropped to sit next to him. I put my hand on his arm in caution and whispered, "I can't talk about it." It actually alarmed me momentarily how my face was only inches from his because I hadn't planned on invading his space bubble like this, and it was a vulnerability for me to be this close to him. However, it was a trade I was willing to make if it allowed him to see the intensity of my anxiety surrounding any talk of my mom.

I could see his Adam's apple bob before he offered, "I don't mean to pry, but I do feel like I can help you."

I was forced to ask, "How can you help me?"

"Do you remember how I shared with you before how I struggled with mental health issues?" His voice trod lightly, opening up the sensitive subject for himself.

I felt the skin between my brows tighten, having forgotten about when he had confided in me about his struggles. Great, now I had guilt creep into my gut because I had probably offended Wally by some of my comments. "I remember now that you brought it up," I said in a low tone even though my throat still felt pinched because I hated this conversation.

"I know you probably don't want to hear it; I'd like to sort of throw it out there that *we* know about the anguish we cause everyone. Most of the time, the avoidance we do isn't about the lack of caring about the other person. It isn't about the other person at all . . . It's because we feel a lot of shame. It's self-loathing that causes us to retreat and avoid."

My eyes skirted away from his so fast, I instantly regretted that I had settled in to sit so close to him because now he had me trapped. Unless I wanted to run out in a fit like a schoolgirl, I needed to reply to him with something. I didn't think it was fair for him to compare his mental health issues with those of my mom because he had never even met my mom. For the entire time I'd known him, he was functional and for the entire time I could remember my mom, she was never functional. I wasn't an expert shrink, but I could easily diagnose the two illnesses as opposites in severity. If Wally knew that my mom could overcook her whole neighborhood and not see she was beyond salvageable, then there wasn't anything I could do to make him see how bad her situation was. "It's not the same," I said. "You're way more normal than she is."

"*Now.*"

I hated the way his eyes dug into mine, because Wally was usually more space conscious with his demeanor. Something had obviously gotten into him. I gritted my teeth and asked, "What does that mean?"

"It means I've been through a lot of stuff." He ran a hand through the side of his hair, partially flattening out some of his natural waves. "I could write a book, but the reason I bring it up is because I can feel how personal you take your mom's behavior. You say it doesn't bother you, but it's the little things you do like muttering under your breath that give you away. You're totally trapped by it."

A cold wave of sweat surfaced on my lower back. I was not sure where it had been hiding but it added to the uncomfortableness of this conversation. I was going to deny what Wally was saying, but my lips stumbled before my brain could stop it, and I heard myself squeak out, "It sucks."

"I know." his voice smoothed over my comment.

"I don't think you do." I could feel my breath building behind my weakened voice, giving it a new surge of power to speak my words more boldly. "I think it sucks that my mom has never once reached out to me to see how I'm doing."

His head rose and lowered, but I didn't stop to let him speak. I could feel adrenaline now fueling my vocal cords and I continued, "It hurts to know that she had been going through something, some sort of depression so badly that she decided to blow up half the town and she never even bothered to call me and ask for help, because you know, I would have helped her. Or, I would have tried. She doesn't let me help her. She never has let anybody help her." I licked my lips but I wasn't done. "It sucks to care about her because I'm the one who always ends up feeling like something is wrong with me and then I'm broken."

He put his hand on my back to comfort me, silencing my frustrations. When I had finally raised my eyes back to meet his, I could see he was unguarded and the look of shame on his face sent a tsunami wave of embarrassment back through me. I understood I didn't have to tell him how I felt because he was gravely aware of the hurt he had *caused* in his life, and he was allowing me to see his flaws so that I could maybe understand a little bit of what my mom might also be going through. "How come you seem so normal?" I asked with more empathy than suspicion.

"I've done a lot of work on myself and for me . . ."

"That doesn't make sense," I rambled out. "My mom has been getting treatment her whole life. Why didn't it work for her?"

"Just because she is in treatment doesn't mean she is working on herself. To me, it seems like she is hiding more than she is healing."

His words rang in my ears so clearly, I knew it was the truest thing I had heard about my mom in a long time. I was reminded of how my dad had said that we can take her to get help, but she has to be the one to actually receive it. I respectfully closed my eyes, trying to bandage the agony that still throbbed when I thought about my dad. Careful not to dwell on the emptiness he had left in my heart, I quickly reopened my eyes, feeling like I was letting my heart hang exposed when I asked, "What am I supposed to do?"

"You need to forgive her and then give yourself permission to love her in spite of her issues. Then you can let go of the feeling that her actions—or lack of actions—are connected to any of her feelings toward you. It has nothing to do with you."

I inhaled deeply. I wasn't used to seeing a serious side of Wally, and aside from piquing my interest in his past transgressions, I was grateful he had opened up to me about this because in a weirdly cathartic way, I felt it helping. I mean, at this point, I had tried about everything else. Why not listen to Wally? I asked myself. I knew something had to change because I could feel a roadblock in my heart path, and I knew if I ever wanted to be fair in my relationship with Fulton, I was going to have to deal with this mamma drama. "Can I ask you something personal?"

"I thought we already were."

"I think you are right when you say that you can see how the way my mom treats me affects me. I can tell it makes a difference in my ability to trust and . . . stuff. Um." I could feel my brows bend inward as I formulated my questions. "How come you don't have any of those issues?"

Wally tilted his head to the side, quizzically. "How do you know I don't?"

I shrugged one shoulder. "I don't know, but you

seem so open to pursuing a relationship with Becky and you barely know her. Doesn't it scare you?"

His pupils flashed a light of recognition my words didn't disclose but he echoed my intentions perfectly by saying, "Are you asking about Fulton?"

I double blinked. "I think so," I said a little reluctantly, still surprised by how honest I was being with him.

"I think it's the role reversal. Like, since I'm the one with the mental health issues and my family, especially my parents, have always been there for me, I've never been the one to personally feel ditched. Whereas in your case, you were the one supporting your mom and not getting anything in return—"

"I get it," I cut him off, now feeling a tinge of jealousy toward him. Then all of a sudden, it was like I remembered again that I was talking to Wally—*my boss* —about my personal life. I stood up, brushing my hands on my pants like I was trying to discard the last ten minutes, and said, "Woo. Tough stuff. Thanks for the chat—"

"Abs." It was his turn to cut me off when he stood up, following me. "Don't be embarrassed."

"I'm not." I headed back to my box, and then I thought out loud, "I wonder why Bre hasn't showed up. Is the door locked?"

"No, it's still open," Wally said as he continued to follow me, but I was doing everything I could to let him know I was *done* with our bonding time.

I stretched my neck to see the exit but there was no one out there. "I better call her because it's way later than the time we agreed on. Something could be wrong with her." Grateful for the excuse to leave, I headed back to my office to grab my phone, and I pledged to not talk to Wally about personal stuff ever again—no matter how hard he eye trapped me.

Chapter Eight

That night, I set my bed up to binge-watch some of my favorite ballets. With my bag of Hershey kisses center on my lap, I plugged my earbuds into my ears and pushed play on a *Cinderella* performance I hadn't seen in a while. I rolled up my wrappers into tiny silver balls, and anxiously watched Act One unfold with busy towns-people all abuzz about the news of the prince's invitation. When I was a little girl, *Cinderella* was my absolute favorite ballet because I saw a reflection of my own life when I looked at how Cinderella related to her step-mother—we were both stuck. I dreamed of finding my fairy godmother to help me escape, and it was silly, but in a way, it gave me a respite that helped me cope.

Halfway through the show, I realized something I hadn't thought about before. Even after the prince had fallen in love with Cinderella, her stepmother still wasn't able to let go of her hold over her and she certainly wasn't going to willingly let Cinderella go off and be happy and be loved. I'd watched this fairy tale unfold dozens of times, but this was striking a nerve. Wally's words telling me I was *trapped* by my momma drama rang clearly as an overlay to this scene. I felt my jaw drop slightly, seeing clearly—I *was* a modern Cinderella story.

I wasn't in my mom's house, or under her rule by any means but I certainly was involved in a weird mental web keeping me from moving on with my prince. I straightened my back into an upright position, pulling my buds out of my ears. I clearly remembered multiple times when I was little that I told myself that if only my mom would get better and then *we* could be happy. It was evident now; I had placed a condition on my happiness and ability to love years ago.

Another similarity I was able to make was that I had seen Cinderella break away from under her stepmother's trap because her fairy godmother gave her the permission to. Then I had the most astonishing realization yet. I wasn't going to have any fairy godmother give me permission to change. I needed to give myself permission to be happy in spite of my mom's condition just like Wally had said.

My thoughts were interrupted by a giggle coming through my wall. Since it was almost midnight, I knew there was only one person Becky could be on the phone with this late. I slid off my bed, tiptoed to my wall, and pressed my ear against it. I didn't feel bad for eavesdropping because I knew Becky would gladly tell me anything she talked about with Wally. I also wasn't listening for the knowledge of what was being said, but I listened because I was intrigued to hear the inflections of someone who wasn't afraid to fall in love.

Mesmerized like the phantom hearing his first opera, I studied the openness in her voice. I would be embarrassed to have to admit that my right leg had gone numb from the way I was twisted forward, resting my ear on the wall by the time she finally hung up the phone. It wasn't that I wasn't sweet in my comments to Fulton, or that we didn't share intimate conversations because we did. However, that stuff was always hard for me and usually only resulted after a buildup of something bad that I needed to overcome. I never willingly opened my heart up the way Becky did and after hearing how happy she was to be able to connect with Wally like that, my heart pined because I wanted the freedom to love like that . . .

I cringed when I stood, realizing that aside from my numb leg, I had strained my neck a little too hard. I walked to my closet, and dug to the bottom of it, where I had a small box of keepsakes my aunt Kim had cleaned out of my parents' condo after my dad had passed. My favorite of the items was the small scrap book Dad had made for me for my sixteenth birthday. Of course, he had made a big presentation about the book—and at the time I was beyond crazy mad because I'd been expecting a new car, not a stupid book—but now that my dad was gone, I cherished this work of his.

True to his fashion in branding *everything*, he had the pages leather-bound in a hue of aubergine, lighter than usual. I was sure he had issues finding leather in the perfect shade, but he definitely always did the best he could, and his perfectionism showed. My lips curved up at the first picture of him holding me in the hospital. Swaddled in a white blanket, I looked peaceful tucked in his arms. I flipped the page to see another photo; I was a toddler sitting on his knee with an open book on my lap. With one arm, he secured me close to his chest while his other hand propped the book up.

I took a deep breath and licked my finger, ready to turn a page in the scrapbook. This was really as far as I ever got with looking at this book. Knowing the rest of the pictures by heart, I avoided them for years because whenever I browsed through the book, I never saw what was *in* the pictures. I was only able to see what wasn't in them—my mom. I don't think it was intentional that my dad selected photos of only him and me as he never told me it was meant to be a Daddy-Daughter book. The fact that he had also tucked a few photos of Becky and me playing dress-up and, later our cheerleading years, right into the front cover of the book, also expressed his intention was for this to be a scrapbook of my entire childhood, but his perfection left out one elephant-sized oversight—that being my mom.

Wally said I needed to forgive my mom and I knew I could never face her physically, so I flipped the page. I saw a five-year-old me with pigtails and my first bike. A pink and blue princess one—Cinderella. Wasn't that ironic? I retorted. With silver and baby blue streamers and a big squeezy horn; I loved that bike. My *dad* had taught me how to ride it, going for bike rides at night after dinner when my mom was resting.

My eyes washed over the picture and even though my vision was becoming blurred, I didn't need to actually look at it anymore and I whispered, "I forgive you, Mom, for not riding my bike with me." It felt cheesy at first, because I was talking to a picture, and she wasn't even in the photo, but I was tired—no, fed up with feeling this cage around my heart. Still not totally convinced this was going to even help me, but I was also out of options, so I flipped another page.

My first ballet recital: me, standing next to my dad, beaming a smile that I knew was fake because I was worried about my mom. Wearing a perfect ballet pink leotard with matching leg warmers that Linda had actually knitted for me. Sweet Linda . . . who was always trying to gently sub for my mother even back then. I knew it would happen, but I felt my sinuses beginning to congest. I plowed forward. "Mom, I forgive you for missing my first recital." Yep, there were the tears, but I didn't fight them. I knew it was going to have to be a part of the process. I went to turn the page but hesitated and added, "Actually, you missed them *all*, but I forgive you."

Dad must have had mercy on me putting only sixteen pages in my book—one for each year. The words of forgiveness got easier, but something beautiful also happened. As before I saw only that my mom had been absent, now I saw how my dad had unconditionally been there *every* step of the way because he was in every photo. Awe of admiration fled through my body, causing my head to shake because he didn't have a clue how to raise a daughter, but he never quit.

With the final page turned, I slowly lifted the cover of the book, letting each page fan back to the start like a waterfall of my memories until it was over and I closed the book, noticing my tears had already dried. I wasn't feeling great by any means, but I felt *acknowledged*. Then, tucking my album back into the box, I lifted it up to put it away, but my eyes caught sight of a photo I had missed. It must have been an extra, like the ones Dad had tucked in of Becky and me, and even though I hadn't ever seen this photo, I remembered the day perfectly. I was about nine, maybe eight. My mom had an episode earlier in the day. Linda had picked me up from dance and taken me to their house to stay the night so I wouldn't have to be alone. I was supposed to sleep on the couch, but their living room seeped with late July air and no air conditioning because they used their window air conditioning units in the bedrooms.

Awake most of the night, and crying—quiet, hot tears because I was upset about my mom—I thought everyone was sleeping. However, to my surprise sometime after midnight, I heard Fulton pad down the hall. I'd never forget how he looked wearing his red superhero pajamas because his shirt was a little short, leaving his slightly rounded belly to poke out from the bottom. He had some serious hair spikes going on, but he was never one to be self-conscious about his looks. He never asked if I needed it, but he came over and handed me his favorite stuffed animal—a dragon who he named Bentley—not after the luxury vehicle that most nine-year-old boys would obsess over, but after the scientist who photographed snowflakes. I smiled at the memory of how even back then Fulton was a huge nerd.

After he handed me his stuffed toy, his eyes scurried back to the hall like he was ready to retreat, but I was scared to be alone, so I asked him to stay. He sat next to me on the couch for a couple minutes before griping about how hot it was and then suggested we should go swimming. He had a plan to sneak into Lasker pool in Central Park, our usual swimming hole, since it was close to his house. I had doubted we could get away with it, but I was smoldering in his apartment and going for a night swim was tempting.

He crept around in the dark, packing a tote bag filled with towels and snacks for us. Then we snuck out, ready for our covert adventure. Thankfully, nothing bad happened, but we didn't get to swim. A police officer spotted us as we entered the park. Brand new on the job, he didn't have the heart to rat us out and even admitted he used to sneak out to swim at night too. He bought us donuts from an all-night diner to bribe us to tell him where we lived. Promising he wouldn't tell our parents about our outing, he dropped us back off at Fulton's house right before the sun rose. Then we ninja snuck our way back in moments before Linda awoke, ready to make fresh caramel rolls for us for breakfast.

Fulton and I sat at the table, stifling giggles over our secret as we dug into the rolls, ready for our *second* sugar rush of the morning. I don't know if Linda ever caught on to our escapade or if Fulton ever confessed, but she must have seen something special in that moment because she took our picture. There we were sitting next to each other: Fulton with his a-little-too-snug pajamas and me in my princess nightgown. Looking innocent enough eating caramels rolls, but both hiding a secret we swore we'd both take to our graves.

I flipped the picture over, looking for a date stamp, but there was nothing. I couldn't believe I hadn't seen this photo before. Feeling like my dad had truly sent me a gift, I held the photo close to my heart, feeling a veil being lifted. *Fulton has always been there.* And it wasn't only because his parents forced him to. There were many memories like the swimming escape where it was just him and me. It wasn't until I pushed him away by being mean that he ever stopped being there for me. I felt my lips part in a silent awe as a new understanding of my childhood seeped in.

What I did next, I would never believe even if you had a video recording of me doing it. I told myself he was sleeping but the logical part of my brain knew he would be up studying. I pulled out my phone and it wasn't nostalgia that was driving my actions because I was seeing my present more clearly now than ever before. It also definitely wasn't a weakness because it took more strength than dancing the part of Belle in *Beauty in the Beast,* but my fingers danced across the letters with instructions from my heart and before my brain could order them to stop, I pressed send on a text message that said:

"I love you."

Since it was so late, it felt surreal like I wasn't really texting him, but after a moment, I could see on my screen cursive writing that said he was replying. My heart did a Jete, but before I could move to reply with a "never mind that typo" text, a reply was received that said:

"I love you too."

I'd like to be able to say I cooed but, instead, I panicked, shutting my phone off. Then when I got nauseous from staring at it on my nightstand, I chucked it under my bed so I wouldn't have to look at it, like it was evidence of something from a crime scene. Then I crawled back into my bed, pulling my blankets up, plotting how I was going to explain this tomorrow. Something told me that the fat, clumsy fingers excuse wasn't going to cut it this time. Burrowing further into my blanket, I closed my eyes, but I was quickly inundated with a warm, rush of emotions and I tried not to scream like a thirteen-year-old girl. I was not sure if I I'd ever know the exact number of years I had loved Fulton up until this moment—many more than I would account for, but I knew it was time to admit it—even if I still had a hard time saying it.

Chapter Nine

I awoke the next morning feeling serene and rested until I remembered how last night had ended. Then my eyes popped open, and I jolted out of bed. My fingers were jittery while I dressed, and I avoided my phone like it was an atomic bomb and decided it was best to "accidentally" leave my phone at home today.

Arriving at work before Wally, it wasn't hard to keep distracted because I had tons to do. While I was hanging up the costumes in chronological use, the corner of my eye caught a glimpse of Bre with an older woman who I assumed was her mom. I lifted my chin to greet them. "Bre! I was worried about you last night."

"I'm sorry." Bre continued to walk toward me, but as she got closer, I could see the fair skin around her eyes looked red and puffed.

I dropped the dress I was hanging back into the box and asked, "What happened?"

Her mom cleared her throat, piping in, "It was my fault. We had so many emotions going on at our house last night, I had to pull the plug on bringing her here until we could talk through some stuff." Her mom placed a hand on my forearm. "I'm sorry for wasting your time and not getting in touch with you. It's not normally how we do things."

My eyes bounced from Bre's mom back to Bre, who I could tell was fighting back a new stream of tears. "It's okay," I said softly. "It's not a big deal. I wanted to have you try on your second act leotard one more time because it looked short wasted, but if you have time now, you can slip it on." I scanned my clothing rack, pulling out the leotard for her.

Bre took it eagerly and followed my pointed finger to my office for her to go change. As soon as she was out of hearing range, her mom leaned in, saying, "We found out last night that the Ballet Master at Bre's dance company is immediately closing the doors due to personal reasons. It's been devastating for her since this is her senior year and she's hoping to get a dance scholarship."

I felt my lips pinch together while my brain registered her words. Bre's dance company was my old dance company. Which meant that her Ballet Master had to be Miss Conner, *my old dance teacher.* "Wait," I spoke up, "Miss Conner is closing her studio?"

"She is. She didn't give a formal statement as to why but she just said it was personal. I totally understand her need to step back, but I wish it could have been more gradual . . . for the sake of the girls."

"Interesting." I rubbed my ear because it perplexed me that she would do something that drastic. Miss Conner, of all people should have known what dance meant to these girls. I remembered when I had my dance days abruptly ended, I re-felt all the feelings of exactly what Bre had to be feeling. "Did you check with another company to see if she could transfer?" I asked, trying to help solve the issue.

"I called a couple, but you know how they are. Most of them have registration deadlines and we are approaching spring already, so everyone is winding down."

"Right." I bobbed my head, knowing fully that Miss Conner's dance company had to have over three hundred dancers and those girls couldn't just be absorbed over night into other classes. "There has to be somewhere they could go so they can finish out their season," I thought out loud, then I felt my eye spring open wider with an idea. "Wait, what if they came here?"

"What do you mean?"

"I have a stage they can practice on." I fanned my arm out to show the space before us. "If they want to stay together to finish out the year, maybe we can set up classes here?"

"We wouldn't want to impose." She waved my comment away. "You are already so busy with this production."

"I don't think it will be an issue," I affirmed. "As long as the instructors agree to it. Those girls already know their dances." Before she could talk me out of it, I further insisted, "Really, let me talk to my boss first, but I'm sure he won't have an issue. We can make this happen. It's not fair for those girls to have this taken away like this without a senior performance."

A curious smile crept on to her lips. "I think it could work." She motioned to my closed office door where Bre was still dressing. "I'll be quiet about it, but I'll call the instructors and a few other moms to see if there would be interest in moving classes over here then."

"Good," I agreed just in time because my office door swung open with Bre emerging in her glittery snow fairy leotard. I scurried over to her; with anxious eyes, I checked all the seams by pulling on them from various directions. "I'm not sure what I was thinking," I said, "but it looks perfect. How does it feel?"

She ran a hand over the front of the satin fabric. "It feels great."

"I guess it was a false alarm." Then I swept my eyes back to Bre's mom, offering, "It's a little early for play practice. I don't think anyone will be here for another hour but if you want to hang out for a while, you ladies are welcome."

Bre's mom checked her watch. Then flicked her eyes back at me and said, "I think we'll run to grab a bite to eat, then I'll bring her back."

"Sounds good." I smiled, flashing a wave, and was about to return to my costume rack when Wally strutted up with a daring smile on his face. "What?" I asked accusingly.

His grin grew, and he wagged his head at me. The

delay in information started to annoy me and I impatiently placed one hand on my hip. "What's going on?"

"I should ask you that."

I threw an exhausted hand up in the direction of my clothing rack. "I'm working."

He straightened his face, beaming his serious eyes at me. "Fulton called, sort of in a panic, wondering if you showed up to work or if you had died."

I could feel my face immediately fade into a frown. "Oops."

"I told him you were here, and you were alive. Then I remembered our chat last night, so I thought maybe something happened as a result of that. I said I thought you were going through some stuff."

"What did he say?"

"He said he could tell but wanted me to remind you about the trip to Montana tomorrow."

My lips made a perfect "Oh" but released no sound because with my recent manic activities I had forgotten about our trip. Wally stood attentive, waiting for me to give him a reply. "Thanks." Then before things got weird, I added, "I know it's awkward to field his calls for me, but you have to understand by now that nothing about me is normal, right?"

His mischievous smile confirmed he knew my truth while I laughed a nervous pattern. He held a confirming hand up. "So, you're good with everything else then?"

"Oh." My voice sprang with enthusiasm. "The dance company I get my dancers from is closing. The owner freaked out for an unknown reason that she never disclosed, and the girls are devastated." The look on his face was unamused, as he prolly found it confusing as to why I would bore him with dance company gossip, so I spoke faster to get my request out. "I promised one of the moms I would ask you, but would you mind if we move classes here? It would be just a few months until the end of their school year." I flashed so much cheese in my smile, I thought I heard mooing.

His head angled, one eye lowered, and he repeated, "Classes?"

"Yeah," I spoke briskly ready to downplay how much activity would actually be involved in absorbing all these classes into our building. "I don't have an exact figure yet, but you don't have to worry because I'll do all the work to coordinate the classes, so they don't overlap with any of the current content we already have." Then I batted my lashes, and added, "Of course, the parents will compensate you for the use of the space. I'm not sure yet again on any figures, but we'll work something out and I promise it'll be lucrative for you."

"Why do I feel like I'm missing something?" His eyes locked on mine. "It sounds like a reasonable enough request . . . but the way you're asking, I feel like you're excluding something."

"I'm not," I insisted. "It'll be totally cool and profitable for you."

"You seem nervous, which isn't normal, and it makes me think something fishy is going on," he reiterated.

"Okay," I breathed out. "Truthfully, it's going to be a lot of girls and it might be a tight squeeze to find room. This isn't the best set-up for something like that, but I felt so bad for the girls, so I offered before I really thought about it, but I swear I'll do my best to make sure the extra activity doesn't overwhelm you."

"Okay."

"Okay?"

"Yeah, I trust you."

A smile overtook my face. "Thank you."

"You're welcome." He turned to leave me but called back over his shoulder, "Call your man so he stops bugging me."

"Ugh."

"I can tell him that."

"Don't."

"Then call him!"

"Okay," I reluctantly agreed, knowing I would call him but not right *now*.

Chapter ten

My heart thumped against my ribs when I climbed into my dad's frog truck parked at the airport parking lot, waiting to give us a ride to the homestead. "I can't believe your parents held on to it," I exclaimed, feeling nostalgic as I slid all the way over on the bench seat to sit next to Fulton.

Fulton felt around under the front seat looking for the set of keys his dad had stashed. "It's a good work truck."

"You could never leave an unlocked pickup in New York."

"Nope, you could not." Fulton turned the key, and the familiar sputtering rumbled under our seats. Then he looked at me. "Are we ready?"

"As much as I'll ever be." I gave him a toothy grin, exposing how much I was forcing myself to go through with this trip. Somewhere deep down, my heart knew he appreciated it even though I'd much rather spend the weekend alone. With his hand of support on my knee, I watched out my passenger window the distant mountains grow closer while we ascended into the rural territory that led to our former homestead. There was something about looking at the scenic views—knowing that this time they wouldn't trap me—that gave me permission to enjoy their beauty much more than I ever did. "I honestly don't remember it being this majestic," I commented when the last of the pale winter sunset disappeared behind the peaks.

I thought he'd agree with me, but instead, he hit on a completely different conversation, one I was trying to avoid. "So, we made it to Montana without talking about our texts. Did you want to say anything—"

"Nope." I spoke over him.

He chuckled, letting his eyes—mossier today than hazel—land on me. "You're something else." I could tell he was watching me as best as he could while also trying to stay on the road, but he didn't pry again. I was in a mood to be quiet, staring out my window even though now it was mostly dark and there wasn't much visible past the immediate ditch.

"I don't know," I started but then stopped. I felt bad for being so barricaded because I could tell he was hanging on to every noise I made, waiting for me to at least acknowledge what we had said.

I attempted to explain again, but this time we both started speaking at the same time. I said, "No, I was actually thinking about that night—"

And Fulton said, "There's something I want to talk

to—" Then we both halted our thoughts with Fulton insisting, "You go first. What were you saying? What night?"

"I had found a picture that my dad had saved. Your mom must have printed it off for him years ago, but I had never seen it. It was tucked away in a scrapbook. It was you and me eating caramel rolls at your parents' house in New York, after that night we tried to go swimming."

I knew the exact moment he recalled the memory, because a tiny sparkle gleamed from the corner of his eye. "That was a long time ago, wasn't it?"

"In a way, it feels like yesterday." I sighed, remembering that when it came to some things, nothing had really changed—like my mom drama. "Up until that night, I thought you were so innocent but no, you were a rebel, sneaking out, breaking into swimming pools," I teased, trying to lift my mind away from my mom. It had been a long time since Fulton and I had any real time to hang out without classes and work and not wanting my mom drama to ruin it, I placed my hand on top of his that was still resting on my knee to try to soften the mood.

Then he added, "I was on a mission to make you smile that night."

"I think it worked." Feeling grateful to have him by my side, I was in awe at the thought of how my life had changed so much since the first time I took this trip up the mountain road. Not only was Fulton now my boyfriend, but he was truly my best friend. The fact that we had grown up together left so many little moments for me to reflect on, but now even little things had new meaning. I continued with my memory, "I remember being devastated, wondering how I would ever feel happy again and then I looked up and there you were, looking adorable in your jammies with your belly sticking out and a stuffed dragon."

"Don't hate on the jammies. I think the belly shirt served a purpose that the lack of air conditioning couldn't." He chuckled, but I couldn't even bend a lip.

I was serious when I continued, "I don't know if I ever thanked you for that night. I'm sure I didn't, but thinking back, it meant a lot to me." I waited for him to look at me again from his side view and when he finally did, I repeated, "Thank you."

"You're welcome." He winked, then quickly locked his eyes back on the road as it winded down into a valley. "I heard you crying," he admitted softly. "I thought you'd eventually cry yourself to sleep but after a little while, I couldn't handle hearing it. I guess I wasn't thinking about getting in trouble as much as I was thinking about helping you."

My lips pulled apart slightly. "You heard me cry?"

He nodded but didn't add anything.

"That I didn't know."

"It's okay," he said softly. "I have super hearing. I can hear a fly fart."

I knew he was trying to get me to laugh, but I felt a little embarrassed knowing he had heard me cry. Even though it was years ago, in a way it felt not that long ago and in many ways it was still very raw. Slowing, he turned into the private drive, creeping along the loose scoria, careful not to throw a bunch of it back up at us. Then he pulled the truck into the clearing and parked, leaving the engine on with the dash lights glowing to light the cab. "Are you sad now?" His eyes scurried across my face.

I was terrible at hiding my emotions from him, so I didn't bother when I simply said, "Nah, not really sad. Sort of sober."

"Sorry, I didn't mean to bum you out."

"It's okay. I'll get over it." I motioned to his parents' house. "And we're here."

"Yes, we are." He took the keys out of the ignition and opened his door, saying, "I'll grab our bags if you want to wait a second."

I leaned forward before he could hop out and called, "Wait, wasn't there something you had wanted to talk to me about?"

Even in the dimly lit pickup cab, I could see his irises tell me that he did have something to say but he retreated. "It's okay." Then he shut his door and walked around the back of the truck for our bags and called out, "It's not a good time."

"It is." I craned my neck, trying to see him, as I called back to him and then waited patiently as he didn't reply.

When he met me at the passenger side of the truck, using one shoulder for our bags and with his free arm, he grabbed my hand again, lacing his fingers into mine, and offered me a coy smile and said, "Later."

My curiosity nudged me to insist we needed to talk about it now, but it was sort of awkward because we were standing outside his parents' house and I knew Linda was probably staring out the window, waiting for us. "Okay," I agreed, walking forward, reminding myself it was only three days. Then the rust-red cabin door burst open, spilling out both Linda and Millie. I hugged them both, feeling their welcome. Fulton placed a hand on the small of my back, nudging me to walk in front of him.

One step inside and I had a strange feeling like I was coming home, even though I had never been in this home before. Everything from their eager grins, to the smells of whatever delicious thing Linda had cooking on the stove greeted me gently. "Your home is beautiful, Linda." I marveled at the way she had in placed the most intricate décor in every nook. I dared myself to find something that was left untouched, but I gave up when I discovered that even the bookcase at the end of the hall was illuminated with a brilliant vintage lamp.

"It's been nice having the extra space," she admitted. Her complexion had a rosy glow and she kept stealing looks at Fulton, who was now freely following his nose into the kitchen. It was sweet to stand back, observing the way the two of them watched each other. "Come in and sit down." She motioned to the island in the center of the kitchen. "Are you guys hungry?" Then moving in front of the stove where a pot was simmering with a perfect single stream of steam piping off the side of it, she took the lid off and said, "It's Fulton's favorite, chicken tortilla."

"You know I'll have a bowl," Fulton accepted, by belling up to the island. As soon as I pulled out the chair next to Fulton's, Millie scooted in, chatting about her school and all the clubs she was in.

"Wait a second." I held a hand up to stop her chatter. "You get to go to a real school in town?"

Linda heard my inquiry and spoke up, "We let her try it out this year because after you and Fulton moved, it was too quiet here. She had her animals, but I could tell she needed peers." She smiled affectionately at her daughter. "It was a trial thing, but she's been thriving, and I've enjoyed seeing her become so outgoing."

I turned back to Millie. "Wow, I had no idea you were getting to go into town. That's amazing."

"Yes, and I joined an after-school club for every day of the week, so I don't have to come home to do chores." She giggled while her eyes flicked back to her mom.

"It's true," Linda confirmed. "It's dark by the time I pick her up, but I'm happy she's happy."

Linda placed two bowls of soup on the island. Then reached back to grab one more, placing it in front of Millie, who hunched over it and said, "You know this is my third bowl?"

"It's fine," Linda dismissed. "Give him ten minutes and I'm sure Fulton will have you beat by a bowl or two."

I glanced at Fulton, expecting him to be deep into his bowl, but he was barely dipping his spoon in. Instead, he was fixed on his mom when he asked, "So, Mom?"

"Yeah."

"Abs and I were talking about something. Did you

ever know when we were in New York, we snuck out to go swimming in the middle of the night and we got caught by a police officer?"

Her eyes widened and bounced to me. "What is he talking about?"

"It's true," I confessed. "That time I stayed the night after you picked me up from dance. Fulton made me sneak out—"

"I didn't make you," he cut in, laughing. "You willingly went with me."

"Well, it was crazy hot in there and it sounded like you knew what you were doing. You were the bad influence."

"Wait," Linda spoke over us. "Are you talking about that time when you were only like nine years old?" Fulton's eyes darted to mine, but his lips were pressed tightly together. Then Linda put a hand over her heart. "Can you imagine if I had known you two were out? It's lucky nothing happened."

"It was fine," I reassured her. "We never made it to the swimming pool. And the policeman who found us bought us donuts and brought us home."

Linda's eyes seemed to shine while she studied her son. "I had no idea. You were always a good kid. If all you have in your past to confess to me is sneaking out to go swimming, then I'd say we did a good job."

Then a breeze wafted in from the front door while it swung open, Eddie appeared, wearing so many layers of flannel, I swore he could fill a whole clothing rack. His eyes beamed when he saw Fulton. "You made it!"

"We're already done with our first round of soup," Fulton said, standing to give his dad a hug.

When he was done hugging Fulton, Eddie took a step toward me, extended an arm, and gave me a side hug. "Welcome back. It's been a long time."

"Thanks, it feels good to be back," I said truthfully, because even though I had been riddled with anxiety about this trip for days, I was feeling okay now.

"Linda's been decorating for days." Eddie flashed Linda a playful smile. "I think she thought you guys were near-blind with all the lights she put up."

"I'm excited to have you guys home," Linda confessed. "And I wanted you to be comfortable."

"Comfortable?" Eddie muttered with an air of teasing, "You better have brought your sunglasses."

Linda flung a dish towel at Eddie, flapping it across his leg. "Stop it," she said, but it was evident she didn't mind the comment because her eyes sparkled back at him.

"Did you see the tree in the family room?" Eddie asked with a raised eyebrow.

"No, I didn't," I replied.

He held his hands up in a stopping motion to get our attention, then said, "You gotta come. I can't believe she didn't show it to you."

"Is it that special?" Fulton asked, his eyes whisked to his mom.

"I just wanted everything to be perfect and since we didn't get to celebrate Christmas together this year, I left the tree up and I have to say it's beautiful."

I stood, pushing my chair back, saying, "Let's go."

Eddie led the way down the hall. "I'm not sure how the lights didn't mess with your plane when you flew in—"

"Stop it," Linda cut him off, chuckling, but she didn't defend herself further because by this point, we were standing in front of the live evergreen that had to be fifteen feet tall since it nearly brushed against their cathedral ceiling. I swore there was an ornament for every branch and the lights were so densely populated that when I squinted, they melded together, making it look like one giant light.

"How did you even get that in the house?" Fulton asked, with a look of amazement on his face.

"I used a crane to get it into the yard and then it took me and another guy to bring it in."

"I believe it," Fulton admired.

I didn't have anything to say because I was so touched by all the time Linda had spent on the details of each little bow. I knew the tree wasn't just about Fulton and me not being here at Christmas, but we were part of it and every where I looked, it was so evident that Linda had gone out of her way to make us feel welcomed, and I couldn't help but feel awestruck.

After the tree unveiling, I mostly stayed quiet, studying the ornaments on the tree while Fulton and his parents spent time catching up, and everyone got plenty of giggles in. Before long, we were yawning more often than laughing and it became obvious we all needed to head to sleep.

Linda made her rounds, shutting off all the lights before coming right up to my side. "Well, let me know if you need anything, but I'm heading to bed too." She turned to leave, but noticed Fulton wasn't leaving for his room, so she gave him a teasing grin. "You two better not think you're going swimming tonight after I go to bed."

We both laughed and Fulton said, "If we had a hot tub, that would be tempting, but I think zero degrees is my cutoff for outside swimming."

She leaned in, hugged Fulton's neck, said good night one more time, then headed to her room. I could tell Fulton had something on his mind, and I tried to give him my attention, but my eyes were literally closing on their own. "I'm so exhausted." I yawned and pulled a throw blanket up close to my neck, snuggling into my spot on the couch.

"I know you're tired, but I wanted to make sure you're doing okay. I know my family can be over-whelming."

"I'm fine. I had a blast. Really, too much fun," I assured him. "What about you?" I knew he was having fun because I hadn't heard him laugh so whole-heart-edly in a long time, but I mostly asked because he had asked me.

"I'm having a good time, but there's something I sort of wanted to talk to you about."

"Oh yeah." I remembered he had promised to talk to me about something. I sat up straighter to try to force myself to awaken. "What's up?"

Then he came around, sitting next to me on the sofa, wrapping his arm around my shoulders. I quickly nestled into his side, resting my cheek right upon his chest. The woodsy scent of his shampoo or something wafted under my nose, inviting me further into the warmth of his aura. I was so comfortable, melded together in his mellowness, I felt my eyes drift closed.

Somewhere in what felt like the distance, I could hear him say, "Yesterday, I spent the day getting all my application packets ready for vet school. I wanted to have everything lined up for when I get back. It was sort of fun in a way to think about all the ways things could unfold, but then I started wondering about you . . ." His words were spaced and more broken than normal, like he was trying hard to string them together. Then he added, "You know, I plan to go to vet school next year. We haven't talked about what your plans are for next year. Do you see yourself doing anything different?"

I arched my head back to get a better look at him, a little confused before responding, "I don't have plans to do anything different. I mean, it was hard enough for me to get the job I have without college." I scrunched my nose up. "Are you wondering if I want to go to college too?"

He shrugged the shoulder I was laying on. "Or whatever. I didn't know if you had talked with Gabby to do anything with her. I'm just curious."

I rubbed the back of my neck, trying to think, but I was honestly so tired I was using all my focus to keep my eyelids open. "I think unless something bad happens, I'll be doing what I'm doing."

"That's what I thought," Fulton said softly. "I was sort of curious like what would have to happen for you to change what you're doing?"

I squinted, using the last little bit of energy I had to stay awake. Even though I could hear what he asked, it made no sense to me. "I'm confused. Are you worried about my mom?" I blinked a couple of times. "Wait, do you know something about her?"

"No, I don't," he immediately affirmed. "It's nothing like that. I was thinking it's hard to make plans for grad school because I don't exactly know where I'm going to get accepted, and I wasn't sure how you would feel if I had to move *away* from New York. I didn't know if you'd be wanting to stay in the city, or if you'd be willing to go . . ."

"I'm going to stay," I cut in. "It makes sense for me to continue what I'm doing. You can go to school, and we can see each other like we do now."

He blinked a few times like he was frustrated but Fulton never got mad, so I ignored it and assumed he was tired too. Then he continued in such a soft voice, I could barely hear it. "I appreciate your confidence in me —and how you assume that I'll get into my top school— but there is a *chance* that may not happen, and I'll have to go out of state."

I still didn't understand why he was hammering this out now. "Then you go where you need to go. Right?"

"That would be okay with you?"

"I don't see why it wouldn't be."

"So, you'd want to do a long-distance relationship again . . . for four years?"

Not really thinking about it, I spoke through a yawn, "We did it before when I was in France."

"Right. But that was only a few months and you had

accepted that job before we were even together. I feel like this is different. Like I'm excited about grad school until I think about what happens if I have to move away from you." He latched his eyes down on mine, giving me a look I could only describe as heart-stopping. "I can't even begin to think about being away from you for that long."

"I don't know why we are even talking about this." I felt my face knot, but there was a root of fear taking hold of my heart from the way he was looking at me and I spoke quickly to try to smooth this conversation over before we both got stressed out. "You have a perfect GPA. There is no way you aren't going to get accepted into an in-state program."

His face stiffened, sending off a vibe like he was shutting down. "You know me. I'm a super planner."

"I know," I barely whispered because my eyes had closed again. Worn out from traveling, and the emotional roller-coaster of this whole trip, I couldn't resist falling into a haze of light sleep. I was going to reply that he was going to do fine, and we'd be fine, but I was fairly sure I was already dreaming of a wonder-land mountain village where only good things happened, and it smelled amazingly woodsy.

Chapter Eleven

The aroma of cinnamon and coffee perked me awake even though the house was still quiet while everyone—well everyone except for Linda—rested. A little chilly from the morning air, I roamed into the kitchen to settle both my need for warmth and my stomach's need for flavor. "Morning," I said through a yawn when I found Linda right where I knew she would be.

With her honey-colored hair still set in old-fashioned pin-curls, she looked up from her project of rolling dough into what appeared to be pie crusts. "Good morning. Did you sleep okay?"

Stretching my arms high over my head, I sleepily answered, "Like a rock. I don't even remember trying to go to sleep and I'm pretty sure I nodded off while Fulton was still talking to me."

Her chin dimpled and she pointed to the counter

where a coffee maker was sputtering out the last few noisy drops of coffee. "Help yourself."

"Thank you." I accepted her offer and walked over to the counter, retrieved a cup, and filled it. Then I turned back to her and asked, "Do you need some help with your pies?"

She kept her eyes steady on her dough as she rolled it another pass and said, "Only if you want to."

"Well, I'm not the best at rolling them out, but I can add the filling." I slid the first pie crust in front of me. "What kind of filling does it need?"

"That one is going to be a sweet potato pie—Millie's favorite." She turned the page on her recipe book and handed it to me, letting her finger guide my eyes and said, "It's the simplest recipe in the world. Just follow these instructions."

Scanning the recipe for a fast second, I quickly agreed, "I should be able to manage that," and then I went to the fridge to get the milk. As I measured the correct amount, I said, "Thank you so much for inviting me this weekend. I know it had to be a lot of work to host, but everything is lovely, and I appreciate it."

"You're welcome." A warm smile grew on her lips, and I knew she was trying to stay humble, but I could tell she appreciated my noticing how much work she had put into the weekend. Then she added, "It's my pleasure."

The patter of feet rushing into the kitchen drew our attention to the door, where we saw Millie sprint up behind me, ready to join the preparations. Then together, the three of us, spent most of the day baking and preparing for the evening meal. Fulton stayed busy outside, helping Eddie with a few farm projects. For the most part it was a lovely day that I didn't mind all that much.

After the evening dinner dishes had been cleared and the table had been wiped, Millie quickly moved to retrieve a stack of her favorite board games, placing them center on the table. "What do you want to play, Abs?" she asked, her charisma bubbling from her round cheeks. "Or we can always get dice or cards out too."

"Anything you want—"

"Actually," Fulton cut in, standing up from his chair at the table. "You've had Abs *all* day while I was outside. I was hoping I could steal her for a little bit." His eyes invited me just as much as his words. "Do you want to go for a walk or something?"

My eyebrows peaked as my eyes shifted to the window to see flurries of snow whisk by in a mostly horizontal pattern. "Isn't it like two degrees and blizzarding outside?"

He gave me a good-natured nudge on my shoulder and corrected me. "It's twenty with light wind."

I glanced briefly at Millie, whose smile had now drooped, which made me want to invite her too, but when I looked back at Fulton, he was giving me an urgent just-say-yes look, tipping me off that something was up, and he didn't want Millie to tag along. "Um, sure," I answered slowly, then turned back to Millie and said, "I'd love to play a game with you in a bit after we get back from our walk. Does that sound okay?"

"Yeah, that's fine," she said a little woefully, making

me smile more because it was cute how much she wanted to spend time with me. I did feel bad for her, though, because I remembered clearly how painfully boring being on the ranch had been when I was here. I made sure to reassure her again that we'd hang out and then I geared up my winter clothes and waited for Fulton, who seemed to now take forever in his room.

Just when I was about to give up on him to start a game with Millie, he finally emerged with a flashlight in one hand and a flannel blanket in another.

I pointed to the blanket with a sharp finger and lowered my eyelids into a narrow gaze as I followed him and said, "It's too cold for a picnic."

He chuckled as he led the way through the front door, and when he reached behind me to pull the door closed, his arm brushed against my back, and I welcomed his touch by scooting in closer to him. "Yes, it is too cold for a picnic," he picked up on my thought, "I think my butt would freeze to the ground if I tried to sit on it." Then he whipped the blanket open with an upward raise of his arms and swung it around to wrap his back like a cape. "It's extra wind protection," he explained as he lifted a corner for me so I could crawl under it like a wing.

Without hesitation, I crawled in and took the opportunity to tease him. "I thought you said there wasn't any wind?"

He flashed a grin that said he *might have* fudged the truth a little to convince me to come out, but I didn't care because I thought it was cute and as much as I didn't hate spending time with his family, I did want to hang out with just him too. We didn't have a plan, but we started to trudge through the snow, together in our shared blanket. Our steps were out of sync, tossing each other around like a couple in a three-legged race. His lips twitched once before laughter tumbled out and it wasn't long before I joined in his laughter, blending in my lighter trill. We didn't give up though and eventually we found our rhythm and when we did, our laughter ebbed, but our smiles lingered and I started, "So, you didn't want to play board games?"

"No, I'll play later, but I wanted to talk to you first because I feel like my mom and sister hogged you all day."

"I actually had a lot of fun with them, and your mom was being so sweet."

"It's definitely her element," Fulton replied in agreement, but his tone sounded more conflicted. "However, it did make me sad to see how eager Millie was to hang out with you because it's obvious she's lonely here."

"I got the same vibe." I lowered my eyes to the snow, watching our feet imprint as we continued to clear our own path in the untouched powder. "However, I'm glad your parents are at least letting her go to school. She's been on this farm a long time and I know I would have never survived."

"I should make more of an effort to come back home to visit. Maybe . . ." Then his voice trailed off abruptly.

"Maybe what?"

I tried to get him to revisit his thought, but his eyes flicked away momentarily before saying, "Nothing. I was thinking out loud." By now we had reached the end of the yard, so unless we wanted to go beyond this mark and get into the waist-deep snow, it made sense to stop so without talking about it, we both simultaneously halted our steps and turned toward each other. Fulton's eyes flowed back over the yard to the path we had taken and then he asked, "Do you want to see the new barn?"

"You brought me out here to see a barn?" I asked as flatly as I could even though I was actually curious to see the new addition because we'd never had anything that fancy when I had lived here.

"No, I didn't," he defended, "but it's a little warmer in there and Millie has a new set of puppies that are super cute."

"Well, in that case"—I tilted my head in the direction behind the house and said— "let's go."

Skillfully pivoting our shared blanket, with the help of a few newly learned hand signals, we headed back behind the house where I found it insanely weird to see the farm like this under the moonlight. With the snow and the feel-good Christmas vibes in the air, I didn't hate it and that was blowing my mind. Well, and the fact that I knew we'd be going home the day after tomorrow helped me to not hate it even more.

Fulton pulled back the rolling barn door, and we entered its darkness with the flashlight sweeping through the blackness. Then we crept up on our hands and knees to peek at the nest of puppies all twisted up into a snuggle pile that centered on their mama dog, who rested in the middle.

"They are so adorable." I infused my whisper with a coo.

"Millie's pretty proud of them."

"I want to snuggle in with them."

"We can come back out in the morning if you want to see them awake—" He bit his lip sharply ending his words and we both ducked down at the same time as the littlest puppy began to move, stretching his hind legs all the way back, then used them to scoot his body forward, further into the pile while his eyes remained closed. We stayed quiet for a long pause to make sure we didn't wake him further. When Fulton was satisfied the pup was sleeping, he let his eyes tell me he wanted to talk and led with, "So."

"So . . ." I echoed his super-serious tone and tucked my leg up under me and leaned back resting on my arm so I could look at him better without having to strain my neck.

I could tell by the way he hesitated to look at me that something was bothering him and when he finally did speak, his random question only further solidified that he was bothered by something. "Are you having a nice time?"

"Yeah . . . I said I had a good day." I let my eyes rest easy on his. "You don't believe me?"

"I believe you, but I was checking."

"I'm fine," I assured him and then added, "Serious-ly," just to cement it in.

"Good. I'm glad. It's been cool to see you with my family. I think they are actually more excited to see you than me, but I totally understand why, so I can't complain." I could tell by the way he deflected his attention again and stared off ahead that he was thinking, but before I would inquire about his thoughts, his words came out in a rush, "I wanted to finish our conversation from last night."

"I fell asleep while you were talking. Sorry." I cringed, feeling guilty for not apologizing earlier. Then I added, "I was so exhausted."

"It's okay." He dismissed my apology, like he didn't want to get distracted from what he was thinking, and he sped right into his concern. "I don't think I did a good job of conveying what I was thinking."

I tried to hide the sigh that I instinctively made because last night's talk about his anxiety about getting into grad school was something I was glad he included me in, but I knew Fulton had a way of over-analyzing things to the point of sometimes driving us both crazy. I didn't feel like rehashing all the what-ifs again and I definitely didn't want his unease to ruin our weekend, but if he needed to be reassured, I would try *again* and I spoke as confidently as I could, "You are going to get into all the best schools, and you have nothing to worry about."

"I'm not worried about getting into school," he stated firmly with his full lips contracting into a thin line.

Now I was perplexed, and I deadpanned, "What are you worried about then?"

"See, I knew you didn't understand." His voice held an air of disappointment, but he managed to let a small grin stumble into place as he continued, "You thought I was worried about school. I'm not. I'm worried about leaving you." Even in the darkness, he wasn't able to hide the intensity of his heated gaze.

"But . . . you're not leaving," I reassured him, casting him a look I punctuated with a quirked eyebrow. "You're staying in New York. You just have to get accepted, which you will."

He shook his head, and it looked like he tried to speak a couple of times before finally saying, "I appreciate your optimism, but there is a *huge* chance I'll have to go out of state. Vet school is the most competitive program, and you don't get to pick. *If* you get accepted, you go where you are selected to go, and you can't complain."

"I get that," I said, now also feeling frustration as my thoughts ziplined back to last night when we had the *same* conversation.

"Right, you're getting that part, but you're stopping there." he said, then slowly continued, "I've been thinking a lot about this——"

"I know," I cut in, sounding more annoyed than I cared to, but his anxiety was starting to edge at my skin like a sharp stone. Then I watched his brows crease with obvious disappointment, so I felt bad and I purposely softened my voice. "You're going to be amazing."

He threw his hands up in the air like he was exhausted. "Again, it's not about school. It's about you. You're not hearing that part." He paused, letting his eyes dig into mine with such intensity, it made my heart thump against my rib cage. "I don't want to leave you. I love you." His whispered confession washed over me and his eyes remained fastened on mine, carrying angst that made me grateful that I was already sitting because I felt a buckle in my knees.

My frozen lips made a silent oh, but no words emerged when I beckoned on them, which was actually relieving because he continued to voice his thoughts with his voice rising half an octave, "I know you aren't one to verbally talk about your feelings and I know that word is hard for you—well, no, *impossible*—and I've been patient and that's cool. We both know how we feel about each other, without having to verbalize it all the time, but at some point, we are going to have to figure out what we're doing beyond the next few months because things are going to change—a lot. If we aren't on the same page, it could get really hard. I want us to be together and to grow together and stop putting obstacles in our own path to happiness."

". . . ah," I tried to come up with a response, but my heart was thumping so hard and so fast and so loud and some other adjective that I didn't even have words to describe. It was obviously in search of the panic button inside my chest as I'd never seen Fulton rant like this—especially about our relationship—and I wasn't sure how I was going to be able to reassure him about his insecurities. So, instead of *once again* reassuring him that he was going to be fine, I took what I saw was the only other route out of this conversation. "I love you too."

His eyes softened, and the stress lines that had stacked on his forehead melted away. Then he leaned in a little closer to me, letting his forehead nudge against mine, and whispered with warm breath, "Was that so hard?"

"Insanely." A surge of adrenaline pumped through my heart, reaffirming what I had said out loud. I lifted my chin, waiting for him to kiss me, but then a sharp pain pulsated up my leg and I found myself wincing, quickly stretching out my leg and nearly shouting, "Leg cramp!"

He flew back, barely missing me kicking him, and as he tumbled his smile took over his face and his unrestricted laughter filled the air. I further pushed my leg out, wiggling my toes. "Ah man! It hurts!" I laughed and then winced and giggled some more. Grabbing my calf, I rubbed the tightened muscle, allowing my body to tuck into a ball and roll to the side, so I was lying like an infant in the hay. "Ouch," I repeated while I rubbed, and Fulton was laughing so hard, his eyes had disappeared into tiny slits.

"I gotta get up." I decided, bracing myself with one hand on the nearest wall. "I need to walk it off." Pulling my lips into a strong grimace, I straightened my leg and tried to move forward. I could hear Fulton still in the middle of a laughing fit and I shot him a mock glare and said, "Glad this is so funny for you."

His eyes brimmed with overflowing mirth when he beamed back at me and said, "You have to admit your timing royally sucks."

"What do you mean?" I hobbled forward a few cautious steps and I started to feel the restriction release.

"Never mind." His shoulders shook, while his laughter continued to brew, filling the space between us as he watched me finish my first lap around. When I managed to circle back to him, he finally was able to fight off the wave of laughter, straightening his face. However, there was a glimmer of humor that still lit his expression when he tried to speak with empathy, "You made it."

"Barely. My toes are so cold I can barely feel them, so I can't really tell where my foot is landing." Then I opened my mouth wide and pretended to scream. "Why do your parents have to live in the tundra?" When I glanced back at Fulton, his lips had just started to quiver into another rush of laughter, which gave me the giggles too, but I maintained a stubborn voice when I said, "I seriously can't feel my toes at all."

"We need to go back inside then because I don't want you to get frostbite."

"We can try, but you're probably going to have to drag me."

"It wouldn't be the first time." A smile etched his words as he moved to close the gap between us and once again wrapped his blanket around my shoulders, pulling me into his aura. In that moment, I had a perfect thought, in that people think that happiness is like a faraway destination, but I knew as we slipped out the barn door back into the night shadows that I had somehow wandered into one of those rare moments in life that forever imprint on your brain when you are later prompted to define happiness.

Later that night, after I had pulled on my fuzzy stocks and snuggled under my blanket, I still felt the burn from my icy toes, but it didn't stop me from period-ically giggling as I drifted into a restful sleep. Having been completely oblivious to how it happened, I now saw that Fulton had not only managed to sneak his way into my untrusting heart, but he had also captured it in all its fullness, melding it right back into his own heart. Not only that, but he had done it in a way that made me convicted that was exactly the way we were meant to be, and I wasn't afraid to love him anymore.

Chapter Twelve

Linda accidentally woke me up when she tried to covertly place a set of hand-sewn Christmas jammies next to my pillow. It was super sweet how she insisted that elves had left them like she was calling on us to mold our hearts to be akin to those of a trusting child who still believed in the magic that is unseen. Just to please her need for Christmas spirit, I pulled my lips into a whimsical smile and gave her a conspiratorial wink when I left her to go slip them on.

They were designed to look like an elf and the shirt had the words: "Honorary Elf" embroidered on it, and I felt pretty good in them and was definitely amused as I headed out to see what everyone else looked like. Once I saw six-foot- tall Fulton, and even funnier, two-hundred-fifty-pound Eddie wearing a similar red and green stripe, I lost my ability to control my rush of laughter.

"I don't think there is anything better than this," Linda declared proudly as she snapped photos of us in all the funniest poses.

I came up behind her and peered over her shoulder, admiring the photo she flashed back at me, but I saw a problem in the picture and immediately suggested a solution. "I think we need hats."

"I didn't even think to make hats but that would be hilarious," Linda agreed, and her periwinkle eyes rounded fuller.

"Do you have any fabric left because I could make a few real quick," I offered, both because I thought it would be hilarious but also because I really didn't have anything else to do.

"Yes." She held up a finger of conviction before spinning on her heel to head back to her room, calling over her shoulder, "I'll be right back." And then she was and so I got busy constructing hats, with Millie hanging out next to me all day, chatting my ear off.

"I have over twenty puppies," Millie explained. Her voice sort of floated right by my ear as I had a hard time keeping up with her random chatter.

"That's a lot of puppies," I said, doing my best to sound genuinely interested. "What do you do with them?"

"I'm a dog breeder, so I sell them."

"It's true," Fulton added from where he sat on the sofa, watching football highlights. "She's made so much money to put into her college savings account from selling dogs that she could probably pay for her first semester at college." He had a proud grin on his face that Millie reflected after receiving his compliment.

"Isn't that a lot of work to feed and clean up after all those animals?" I asked as I repositioned my fabric to sew the last few sides of my final hat.

"I don't mind it," she said. "It gives me something to do, and the puppies are sooo cute." Then we were interrupted by the sound of Eddie singing an altered version of "Jingle Bells." Millie and I got the giggles so badly that I could barely finish my last row of stitches. Eddie had broken into the eggnog at dinner, so by now he was pretty convinced he had the musical chops to sing any Christmas carol that popped into his head. Usually, he was a man of few words. He preferred to be busy with his hands and not his mouth. So, it was extremely hilarious to see him so out of character. I could tell Linda enjoyed his new confidence because she encouraged him to keep singing while she smiled slyly in the corner, with an amused twinkle in her eye.

"Someone needs to record him," Fulton said.

"Right," Eddie loudly agreed. "That way when I'm famous you can all say you knew me when."

"Um-hum," Fulton agreed through tight lips.

"Why don't we open some of these shiny things?" Eddie exclaimed, grabbing a box that was so beautifully wrapped with metallic gold paper and silver bows, that it looked like it should be part of a luxury Christmas display in a department store.

"That is a beautiful package," I commented, looking at Linda because I didn't have to guess who wrapped it. "Actually, they all are."

"I love wrapping presents," Linda explained. "I think it's part of the idea of a gift. I can't stand it when I see a gift, slopped in a gift bag with a crumpled piece of tissue paper sticking out of the top. I mean, what does that say about how you feel about that person?"

"It says you don't want to waste money on wrapping paper," Fulton said.

"No . . ." Linda further explained. "I want my gifts to make people feel special. I find the presentation is the most important part. It's like if you make someone a meal and it looks like mush, and you plop it on a dirty plate and slide it over in front of them. Do you think they would want to eat that?"

"Depends," I said, "on who cooked it. If you cooked it, I'd eat it because you could make mush taste amazing."

Linda's smile widened, but she brushed off my compliment by saying, "Well, you get the point. I want everyone to feel like they are receiving a special gift."

"So does that mean we get to open them?" Millie asked, her eyes glued to the stack of towering presents.

Linda surveyed the room. "I don't see why not." She winked at Millie. "Youngest goes first."

Millie crawled up right in front of the tree and checked each box for her name, and every time she found a box that was hers, she shook it and then set it in front of her. When she was satisfied with her collection, she took the largest of all the boxes. "I'm going to start with the biggest."

"Gather round, everyone." Linda waved us all in

front of the tree. With a camera in her hand, she positioned herself across the room but in front of Millie. "Okay, sit next to the tree instead of in front of it, so when I take your picture, you're not blocking the tree," Linda instructed.

"You're a perfectionist, Mom," Fulton teased.

"I know, but I need something to look back on when you guys are older."

"Can I start?" Millie's hands hovered over her gift like she was ready to dive into a pool to save a drowning baby.

"Yep, go ahead," Linda said. Millie tore through her paper so fast I almost got whip lash trying to keep up with the pieces of paper that flew in all directions. Then she squealed in excitement as she pulled out a new cell phone.

Pumping both fists in the air, she screamed again, "Yes! I got my own phone!"

"It's for when you're at school and you need to get ahold of me," Linda instructed.

"Thank you so much, Mom." Then she looked over at Eddie. "And Dad."

"You're welcome," Linda said. "After we're done with gifts, Dad'll help you set up your preferences."

"That's awesome. Thanks," she said again and placed the gift next to her. Glancing back at the tree, she asked, "Who's next?"

"The next youngest," Linda said. "So, I think that's Abs, right?"

"I think so," I said.

"Oh, I saw one with Abs' name on it," Millie piped in again. She reached back under the tree and went right to a little square box that was wrapped in the same motif that Millie's gift had been wrapped. She handed it to me, and I didn't bother to look at the tag because I knew by the wrapping it was from Linda. I unfolded the paper carefully, taking my time.

"Have Millie show you how to rip it off the right way," Eddie teased.

"It's too pretty to shred into pieces." I pulled a velvet box out of the paper and rotated it, so the front was facing me. The little hinges made the faintest of creaking noises as I flipped the lid open and as my eyes focused on what was inside, I grabbed my chest, inhaling sharply. My senses were disoriented and my eyes seemed consumed by a false ambient light that seemed to gleam from the box. When I finally managed to unglue my eyes from my present, I first sought Linda and asked, "What is this?"

Linda strained her neck to see across the room, and her eyes about doubled in size when she declared, "That ain't from me." The fact that she all of a sudden had a back-country accent that used the word ain't alarmed me a little, but I didn't dwell on it, because it seemed like all the sound in the room was drowned out by the rapid thumping of my heart.

Millie had now slid closer to me to see what I had and when she caught a glimpse of my gift, her face animated and she exclaimed, "It's a huge diamond ring!"

"What!" Fulton's face flushed white as he flew

forward out of his chair. I'd never seen a man move as fast as he did when he dashed across the room, grabbed the box out of my hand, and brought it to his own face for a closer look. Then a moment later, he flashed it back toward me and asked, "How'd you get this?"

My hand was still extended like it was holding the box even though it was now empty because I had become frozen in confusion, but somehow, I managed to let a few words slip out, "It was in the wrapping paper." With disbelief, my face knotted because I didn't think I would have to explain to him how I got it because he had been sitting there the whole time.

His eyes were alarmed, as they fled to the tree, then back to me and then to the stack of wrapping paper that was next to me. His jaw hung so low that I couldn't decide if he was shocked or if he was mad. One thing was for sure, he obviously knew more about the ring than Linda did, so I fastened my eyes on him, and with a shaky voice I asked the question I already knew the answer to, "Is this from you?"

"No." His face was so strained, I decided to keep quiet until he was ready to tell me what was going on. But he didn't know what was going on because he outstretched his arms wide and asked me, "What happened?" Then he paced back to the tree, like he was looking for signs of a clue or something.

"What are you looking for?" Linda finally asked him, now a look of concern gracing her face.

He picked up the paper I had discarded, holding it up so his mom could see. "Did you wrap this?"

She lifted a shoulder like she didn't really care for his

tone but wanted to help, so she decided to talk anyway. "Did you put it in my room with the rest of your gifts you asked me to wrap?"

Fulton bit down on his lip and I could see his eyes grow even more round. "I set it on your dresser because I didn't want Abs to accidentally see it in my room."

"I must have thought it was one of the presents you put in there for me to wrap." She shrugged, saying, "I remember wrapping a little jewelry box and since I didn't have a present that you had marked for Abs, I assumed it was for her." Then she quickly covered her mouth. "Oh no! She wasn't supposed to open it. Was she?"

Fulton's lip quirked when he firmly stated, "Uh, no."

"I didn't know," Linda squeaked out.

"I didn't think you'd wrap it and stick it under the tree! And why wouldn't you look inside to see what it was?" Fulton said more to himself than as a point of argument.

"Like I said, I didn't look inside. You had the other gifts marked with names and I was in a hurry to get everything done by morning." She looked at me with huge, sad eyes. "I'm sorry, Abs."

I was still massively perplexed, letting my eyes bounce from Linda to the diamond ring, which now appeared to be glaring at me, drawing me into a weird throbbing tunnel vision. My brain flashed confirming words in my head telling me what this ring was obviously meant to be, but my heart rapidly stacked a thick brick wall around those words, refusing to believe it. When I looked back at Fulton, there was a white-hot silence in the room. I swear I could hear a faint buzzing from the Christmas lights among of cacophony of noises that normally would have blended into the background. I waited for someone to say something—but no one did, so I finally forced myself to latch Fulton's eyes. "What is it?"

"You know," Linda cut in, "I think I smell something burning in my oven." She elbowed Eddie. "Hon, kitchen." Then she looked at her daughter, saying, "Millie, can you both come help me in the kitchen?" When no one followed her, she turned, urgently waving at her husband, who sat relaxed in his chair like he was ready to open the next gift. "Eddie," she whispered sharply, "my oven is on fire."

He leaned forward like he was sniffing the air. "I don't smell anything."

She opened the door to the kitchen and harshly whispered, "Get over here."

He reluctantly got up, following Millie, and after they had all disappeared into the kitchen, Linda closed the door. I heard Linda loudly instruct them to sit at the table. Eddie must have complained because then I heard Linda tell him to sit down and drink eggnog, but then it was quiet after that. My eyes had followed them into the kitchen, and I had kept them fast on the closed door, but now it was silent. Without anything else to do, I leveled my attention toward Fulton, who was now sitting next to me with the biggest look of disappointment on his face. It felt like an arrow had pierced my heart, "What's wrong?"

He held the velvet box back out, so I could see the

ring. I hadn't gotten a decent look at it before because he had yanked it away. "This was my grandmother's ring," he explained as he took the ring out of the box and then held it out for me to take from him. It didn't take me long to figure out that it was a very expensive ring with an oval diamond in the middle and a single row of tiny diamonds framing the center diamond. The white gold band was textured the way most vintage jewelry was, making it absolutely stunning. "It's beautiful," I complimented as I now fully understood that Linda had accidentally wrapped up a family heirloom and then by mistake put my name on it. I smiled because it was sort of hilarious now to think about what a crazy mistake that was for me to get this ring.

"Why are you smiling?" Fulton's brows sharply bent down, but his gaze steadied on mine as he continued to seek clarification.

"It's funny how it got mixed up into the pile of gifts." I held the ring back out for him to take from me so he could give it back to Linda.

Fulton let out a joyless chuckle before binding his eyes back to mine. "Okay, I'm going to tell you everything."

"Huh?" I now felt lost again and I could feel my forehead crinkle.

"So, this was my grandmother's ring. My mom thought you might like to have it as your ring if we got *engaged* . . ."

Now it was my turn to let out a stutter as I felt a quiver in my chest start to bubble. "W-what?"

"Slow down." Fulton grabbed my hand. It was sort of sweet, but I knew he was mostly doing it to avoid having me fly out of my chair. "I know you aren't ready for this conversation and the timing isn't right, but I don't see any way around it. So, it was just a discussion that my mom and I had. I agreed the ring was beautiful and it's worth way more money than anything I could ever afford. I thought you might like it if *someday* we got engaged." He looked at me with a bit of a sideways look to make sure I was following him.

"Okay . . ."

"She gave it to me to have . . . for you know . . . in case. But I didn't want you to find it in my room, so I set it back on her dresser."

"And then she saw it sitting there and thought she was supposed to wrap it," I finished his sentence.

"Apparently," he said, but he didn't look relieved that the mix-up had been clarified. In fact, I doubted it would have been possible, but he looked even more disheartened.

"Why do you look sad? It's just a mix-up. No big deal." I freed my hand from his, trying again to return the ring to him, but he refused to look at it.

His lips parted slightly before he said softly, "I had wanted to surprise you with it when the time was right." Then he paused, letting his eyes land on mine, and I wished I could say that he saw the humor in the situation and was ready to laugh, but all I saw was deep hurt —actually regret.

I held my hand out and lightly touched his cheek. "I

don't understand why you're so bummed. It's okay. Not a big deal—"

"It is a big deal," he cut me off. "The look on your face when you saw the ring was a look of absolute horror." The corners of his mouth bent down, and he continued, "I know you struggle with the whole concept of commitment, but I wouldn't have expected you to react like that. I would have thought you'd at least be a little excited."

"You totally caught me off guard!" I blurted out, now feeling defensive. "I had no idea what was going on, and we've never even talked about getting engaged, so it seemed completely misplaced, almost like a joke gift."

Fulton had a deep scowl on his face when he declared, "You didn't think it was a joke. You would have laughed if you thought it was a joke."

"Okay," I admitted. "I didn't think it was a joke, but I was massively confused because I thought the gift was from your mom."

"It doesn't matter," Fulton said so softly I had to lean closer to hear him. "I now know how you really feel about getting married."

"Do you?" I felt my brows quirk up like question marks. "Because you never asked me."

"I tried! You know how I kept trying to talk to you the entire time we've been here?"

I narrowed my eyes, like it would help to peel away the last remnant layer of his secret as I accused, "You talked to me about grad school."

"Right." He gave me the most curt nod I have ever seen that it actually made me sputter out a laugh that sounded more like a snort, but he ignored my mocking and went on in an aggressive one, "But the part you didn't hear was that I wanted to tell you that when I leave for grad school, I don't want to leave you!" He paused like he had realized he was shouting. Then he centered his eyes back on mine, and the connection I felt made my gut wrench in all the best ways. Leaning his face closer, and even though he lowered his voice, I still heard a crack in his pitch when he continued, "In my head, it makes sense for you to come with and then in my heart it confirms that I want to get married so we can start a life together."

His words sent a spear right to my heart. They should have made me happy, but this whole conversation was causing my body to tense up. I gave a light toss of my shoulder in a shrug, but I knew it didn't do anything to balance the weight of this conversation that showed in my eyes. "Uh . . . you never said that."

"No, because whenever I tried to hint at how I felt, you seemed so disinterested about having a conversation about *our* future. You kept focusing on our lives as two separate things like how I'm going to do well in grad school, and you never included yourself in that picture."

"So . . . why didn't you just bring it up like we are talking now?"

"Because it's hard." His eyes were wide and centered on me. "I didn't want you to think I only wanted to get married because I didn't want to do a long-distance relationship again. I'll admit it, if it were perfect, I think I'd prefer to wait until I'm done with school, but the fact I'm leaving opened my eyes to what I know is the most important." He paused and then whispered, "Aubergine." I had never heard him whisper my name like that and I honestly was astonished that I couldn't feel a burn from the look he gave me when he said, "I can't even think about leaving New York without you."

My eyes did a tandem blink, and I know this was the part where my heart should have constricted or fluttered or something at how intensely he looked at me, but it didn't because my brain got snagged on one word. "Wait. You just said, you *are* leaving."

His eyes were unflinching. "I've been trying to talk to you—"

I stood up, feeling like I was suddenly being ambushed because this was *new*. He had never said he *was* leaving like it was a fact. Every conversation we had —and there were many—had been breezy and filled with what-ifs. "No." I shook my head violently. "You never tried to tell me that."

He stood up too and reached out for my hands, but I pulled them back. When he tried to put an arm around me to pull me closer, I took a giant heart-stabbing step backward. "Abs, calm down."

"No," I half-shouted. The sound of coughing echoed from the kitchen, reminding me we weren't alone in the house, and I had probably scared the willies out of everyone in the kitchen. I consciously lowered my voice, narrowing my eyes. "How long have you known?"

"It doesn't matter how long I've known because I've been trying to tell you this whole time."

"How long?"

"I'm not sure I remember."

130

"Fulton, be honest."

He tried to grab my hands again and this time, I let him. "I had a plan to tell you, but everything changed when your dad died. I knew I couldn't bombard you with this because you've been so sad about your dad. I couldn't do anything to make it worse."

"How long?"

He licked his lips, then finally answered, "So you remember when I got that letter from the school in Florida?"

"You said it was an early admission thing and you were going to wait to see if you got into a school in state."

He lowered his eyes to the floor, and I knew he had been covering the truth since then. "Actually, it kills me to tell you this—and I hate it—but do you remember me telling you how I went to see your dad before he died?"

"Yeah," I squeaked out.

"He explained to me when I was there that I was going to get this offer and it's been my top pic ever since, but I didn't want to say anything until I knew for sure that Rich would come through."

My heart deflated like a child's balloon stabbed with a pin needle. It had been so full all weekend, feeling all the love and togetherness of Fulton and his family. I would have never guessed it could be drained of all the positive feelings in one instance. "So, you're going to school in Florida?" I asked as flatly as I could.

"I haven't sent my letter off yet because I wanted for us to make this decision together. However, when I do the math, it makes the most sense for me to accept the teaching assistantship. I've been lucky enough that my parents have covered all my undergrad bills, but after I graduate, I'm on my own and I'll be looking at six figures of debt easy by the time I finish grad school if I stay in New York. If I accept the scholarship and teaching assistantship in Florida, I'll make money from my teaching assistantship. It's modest, but I can live off of it." He squeezed my hand, letting his eyes penetrate further into mine. "Actually, we both could."

A cold shudder ran up my spine at the way he so easily included me in his vision.

I turned my head away from him and when I didn't respond, he added, "I'd be able to graduate with little to no debt versus a couple hundred thousand. It seems like a no-brainer." Then he took his hand, placed it on the tip of my chin and gently glided it up my cheek until I caved and turned back to look at him. "Until I think about being away from you for four years. I don't want to leave you. I want you to come with." He lowered his face right next to mine and in a voice barely audible, he whispered, "What do you think?"

"Honestly, I'm more put-off by the fact that you were feeling this and never told me." I pulled away from him so I could see him better. "You know, I can't handle it when you keep secrets."

"I know, but I was waiting for the right time."

"And I can understand that," I admitted. "And you're right. It does make a lot of sense for you to accept that position when you explain it to me like that." I felt my throat pinch as I started to voice the next part, but I pushed forward. "But if you really feel like that's the best option for you, I'll support you."

"But you don't want to come with?"

I was going to talk, but my words wouldn't come out, so I pressed my lips together tightly and shook my head. Then I mouthed the words, "I can't."

"Can I ask why?"

"I spent forever trying to get a job, and I finally got one and I'm happy there. I feel like I wouldn't be ready to leave my life to start over again."

Fulton let out of heavy breath. "I think I already knew that, but I was hoping we'd have like a Christmas miracle where things would be different."

"Sorry," I said softly. "But you should totally go where you need to go and do what's best for you."

"Well," Fulton said, in a lighter voice but I could tell he was faking his tone. "Let's wait to see what other offers I get."

"Yeah." I also now forced a fake inflection and I dared to look deep into his eyes, past the facade he was showing me, and it was obvious he was wounded— which prodded at my heart in more than one way. I was overjoyed for Fulton that he had gotten this amazing offer, but I also wanted to argue that Florida had never been the plan. The plan had always been for him to stay in New York and go to grad school. That made sense. We'd have time to date and figure things out without rushing into things. It wasn't that I was against getting married—eventually. I just always assumed I'd spend my twenties doing my own thing before I'd have to think about settling down. I wasn't ready to commit my whole life to another person, even if it was sweet Fulton.

"So, we are good?" Fulton asked.

"Of course." I smiled, knowing all too well that Fulton wasn't going to be able to forget about this night for a long time, if ever. But it was too late to take it back.

Chapter Thirteen

Not being able to sleep because of the ring drama, I was left with the lingering memory of the disappointment on Fulton's face, and it killed me. I had never wanted him to feel rejected, but I was at least one thousand percent sure I was not ready to get married. However, that had nothing to do with him because I was also one million percent sure that I loved him immensely and couldn't imagine my life without him. After struggling alone with the heartache for way too long, I gave up and quietly snuck down the hall because I needed to talk to him.

However, when I was in viewing range of his room, I was surprised to see a soft light emitting from underneath his closed bedroom door, and the sound of muffled voices escaped from inside. Confused about who he was talking to at this hour, I tucked against the wall, listening closely until I recognized Linda's voice, and it only took a moment longer before I knew they were talking about me. I held my breath and listened, feeling somewhat ashamed. Then I heard Fulton say, "I'm not surprised. I mean, it wasn't at all how I had it planned. Nobody would plan that."

"I'm sorry, hon. I don't know where my mind was when I wrapped that box up."

"It's okay, you didn't mean to." His voice was expressionless in a way I had never heard it.

"But you guys talked, right?"

"Yeah, we talked."

"Did you tell her you want to go to Florida for school?"

"I did, but she wasn't interested in coming with, which I sort of knew. Now, when I think about leaving for school, I dread it. We literally just got in the same zip code this month. I can't even think about going back to the distance thing."

"Well, you'll be busy, and time goes fast." Linda's voice was the perfection of trying to push optimism as she carried on, "I'm sure she can come out to visit too when you have breaks."

"No, Mom. You don't know Abs the way I do. It's not going to work."

"You think she'll break up with you?"

"I think . . ." He dropped out an exaggerated groan that even through the closed door I could tell he was beyond frustrated when he said, "Abs doesn't have a lot of confidence in some things, and she definitely doesn't give herself enough credit. It's hard to explain, but I think that when it would get hard, she would use that as an excuse as to why we shouldn't be together."

"You don't know that." Linda's voice was smooth and warm. "She loves you. I can tell by the way she looks at you. In fact, I even remember seeing that look on her face when she lived here. Although she wouldn't have admitted it back then, but I could tell she loved you. She's loved you for a long time."

"It's not a matter of how we feel about each other. It's a gut feeling that I have that it would be too hard with our schedules. There's no way we wouldn't grow apart being away from each other that long and I could see her using that as an excuse."

"So, what are you going to do?"

"I'm going to stick with the original plan. I'll wait to see if I get into a school in New York and go there because then I get to have both of my dreams."

"Honey, I want you to really think about it before you turn down that offer. You're going to be looking at a lot of debt."

"I know, but that was always the plan. Most people have debt when they graduate. Plus, there is an advantage to staying in New York because the schools are more prestigious, so you can't really compare them by the dollar amount."

"I know you'll do what is best, but really, think about it. It's only four years, but it's a lot of money and it'll take decades for you to pay that back. I don't want you to regret anything."

"What would I regret?"

"I don't know that you would, but I think it's easy to be on this side of it and be optimistic but once those bills start coming, and they prevent you from taking vacations, buying a home and moving on with a normal life, you might wish you would had done it differently."

"I'm going to have to deal with it then," Fulton said. "I can't leave Abs. Especially now after she lost her dad."

"It's not up to you to save her."

"I'm not trying to *save* her. I love her and I want to be with her."

"So, let me ask you this. What are you going to do if you make this sacrifice for her, and she never wants to get married?"

Then there was a silence that was so heavy it sent a sting to my eyes, and I batted my lashes in reflex, desperate to make it stop.

"You never thought about that?" Linda eventually added.

"It doesn't make sense to think about that."

"I know you are being an optimist and I love how you want to be such a great partner for her. She's a special person and she's been through so many horrible things, but I'm not convinced you guys want the same things and that can be a problem. I think you have convinced yourself eventually you'll want the same things, but I have to pull the mom card out and warn you. That doesn't always happen."

"Why would you say that? Are you trying to talk me out of being with her?"

"No, not at all. I've just seen more than a few couples where one person makes a lot of sacrifices, thinking that the other person will *eventually* come around and it doesn't usually happen like that. Usually, people are who they are."

"Right. And I know Abs and I guess I don't care what happens to the money stuff. I know I don't want to do a long-distance relationship, so I guess I'm lucky I still have the option of going to school in state."

"You are lucky that way," Linda said.

"And I also think it's sort of rude how if I would have gotten accepted to an in-state school a month ago we'd all be excited and proud, but now that option seems like it's a huge failure but it's actually not. It's still really amazing to be able to say I'm going to vet school at all."

"You're totally right. I'm sorry if I made you feel like you haven't been successful."

"So, I'm going to stop talking and plan on going to school in New York."

"It's a good plan."

"It's a great plan."

I could tell their conversation was winding down and I didn't want to get busted, so I quickly jetted back down the hall, threw myself onto the couch, and whipped a blanket up around my body so it looked like I had sacked out hours ago. It only took a minute, and I was grateful I left the hall when I did because I heard Fulton's door open. I laid as stiff as I could because I figured Linda would be one of those moms who was always checking on everyone while they slept, but she seemed to go straight into her room. Wanting to go to Fulton and confide to him about all I had just heard, I was about to get up, but then I froze because I knew he would figure out I had been listening to his conversation and I wasn't going to confess that. I knew it wasn't right to listen to it, but it was such an awkward situation, I had to know how he truly felt.

THE FOLLOWING MORNING was a mad rush to get to the airport on time. With the roads slick with fresh moisture, we didn't get up early enough to accommodate the extra time we would need to travel on the slippery roads. The travel reports threatened another foot of snow over the next day, and Eddie hadn't prepared the animals with enough food. He decided to spend the morning bringing the cattle closer to home, so he told Fulton and me to take the truck in by ourselves and he would fetch it on a future trip to town. It seemed like an odd plan, and I still thought it was an excuse to give us alone time to talk more after the uncomfortable night we all had.

The thing with Fulton was that I knew he wasn't going to hold anything against me even if he had gotten hurt. We were awkwardly quiet for the first few minutes as we tried to find something neutral to talk about, but once we did, we managed to have a normal conversation, but it still seemed like we were overly polite in our speech. When we finally got close enough to town to get cell phone reception, our phones started beeping as they received all our missed text messages. I wasn't expecting anything much, but I browsed anyway. "Oh, I got a text from Wally." I felt my brows pull up in interest when I opened it and read it out loud.

FYI – Remind me to tell you we are NEVER using live animals in a production again!!! Some of the cats got out of their cages.

My palm fled to cover my mouth. "Oh no."

"That could be bad." The smile I had been missing since last night seemed to resurrect on his lips, and it sent a pang of relief to my heart because I could see a glimpse of us finally starting to get past the lingering dust of disappointment that had been so thick in the air all morning.

I looked at him over my wrinkled nose grin. "Do you think he's mad at me?"

"Nah, maybe a little annoyed, but if anyone can see the humor in something, Wally can."

I quickly texted back. "Sorry." Then I stashed my phone back into my purse and fixed my eyes on the ditches flying past us out of my window.

After a long moment, I felt Fulton slide his hand over my knee. "What's wrong?"

Joining my hand onto his, I saw his touch as a reassurance that I was needing and I closed my eyes for the briefest of moments before asking, "What makes you think something is wrong?"

His grin was becoming easier for him now as I could tell it even held an air of teasing when he pried, "Because you always monologue stare out the window when you are trying to avoid talking."

I allowed my eyes to gently wash over him to further confirm that I wasn't holding onto anything from last night. "It was just nice to get away from our normal lives for a couple of days. You know, I didn't think about work once. And my other issues, they never crossed my mind either."

He swapped his easy grin for a stoic expression. "And by other issues, you mean?"

I sighed, knowing he was going to bring it out of me anyway. "I guess I was thinking about my mom because I had promised myself I would visit her when I got back to have a late Christmas thing with her." I let my lips twist into a lopsided grin, despite how I literally felt disgusted. However, putting on a stupid mock smile didn't help me to feel better, so I relented and confessed, "I talked to Kim before we left, and she thinks my mom is most likely headed for jail once she gets charged with arson. I feel terrible about it, but then again, I know she did it to herself. Then I wonder what the point is when I know she hates it."

Fulton raised one of his brows in a northerly fashion. "You mean, you are wondering what the point of visiting your mom is?"

"Now, before you lecture me about how she's my mom—"

He cut me off by saying, "I'm not going to lecture you about that at all because I agree with you."

"You do?" My voice leaked out in a weak whimper.

"I agree she's your mom, but it does seem like there isn't much point because you two just make each other miserable."

I held my chest defensively and quickly rebutted, "It's not my fault."

"I never said it was. And I don't think it is. It's a pattern that when you asked the question, what is the point, and my answer was, I really don't think there is one."

Pulling my eyes away from Fulton, I refocused back on the ditch, wondering why I felt the need to visit my mom, and the truth was, I didn't really feel like I needed to see her as much as I felt like I owed it to my dad. He had been so insistent that we needed to love her unconditionally and that meant we had to follow her all over to hold our family together. I didn't want to disappoint him by letting everything he had tried to hold together just dissipate. "I think the point is more about my dad," I admitted softly.

He stole a look at me, and I must have looked pretty pathetic because he instantly squeezed the hand that was still on my knee in an effort to comfort me. I thought that was going to be the end of the conversation because what else could he say to support me when it came to my relationship with my mom? But then he surprised me by saying, "I don't think you should go see her."

My nose scrunched. "What?"

"I think," he started slowly, "that it'll be more of the same, but not."

"How do you mean not?"

"I mean that she's your mom and you've always had to live under her guidance—well, mostly that of your dad's guidance, but he always protected her. However, in your case, I think you're going to be one of those people who needs to transition to treating your mom more like

143

an adult friend and less like an authority figure because she obviously isn't in the mental health to be that to you."

"So, what does that mean?" My too-quick response seemed to linger, but Fulton knew what to do with it and he lowered his voice a notch as he explained it to me.

"It can mean what you want it to, but I know you two don't have a typical mother-child relationship. I think you feel like you still need to do all the things families do, but if she doesn't want to and she never initiates any contact with you, to me, it sort of feels like it does more harm to your mental health—at least for right now."

Thinking about not being there for her tugged at my heart. Even though she never reached out to me, and I knew how messed up that was but still I felt some loyalty toward my dad. I could imagine his face being so let down if he knew I hadn't tried to see her. I turned my eyes back, staring out the window, because I didn't want to risk getting emotional. Knowing I would never give up on her because my dad never did, I also knew Fulton couldn't understand that part. "I can't just ditch her, though."

"That's not what I'm saying."

"Then what are you saying?" My voice dug in, accelerating in speed, but Fulton held his tone steady and didn't match my aggression.

"I'm saying that every time you have to go see her, you get a giant set back. I'm not telling you to ditch her, but I think it would be better if you took some time off to work on yourself so you can live a normal. .

." His voice trailed off like he knew he had said too much.

My eyes widened, because I knew he was trying to reference what happened last night without having to actually say it. But the crazy truth was he did have a valid point. My dad had made it his mission to keep us all together. No one had ever even hinted at giving me permission to take some time off from dealing with my mom's issues to work on myself, but I had to admit the thought was intriguing. "So, how do I work on my issues?"

"I wish I had the answer to that, but I do keep thinking back to something I read when I had psychology."

"What was that?"

"I'm not a huge Freud fan, but he had made the observation that family life is organized around the most damaged person. I remember reading that and instantly seeing your life. I think everything was always about your mom. Your needs, and even those of your dads, went unnoticed. But just because they went unnoticed doesn't mean they didn't matter." We had stopped at the last stop light before the airport and the pause gave Fulton enough time to lock eyes on mine. "Have you ever done counseling by yourself?"

My mind burrowed back through my youth, but it didn't take long for me to confirm, "No. Every time we went to counseling it was always with my mom or some other form of family therapy where we were there supporting her."

His lips pushed out before he finally said, "I think I'd

start there." Then the light changed, and he turned his head back to the traffic, leaving me to stare at his side profile.

I knew he was right. In fact, I think I had always felt like I needed that, but my dad had always been so busy with my mom's issues that the way I could make it easier for him was to stay in my lane, pretending I was fine. Unless my issues were something physical that he could see, like a dance injury or a bad grade, he stayed oblivious to anything deeper than surface level. It wasn't his fault because he was always struggling to hold everything together. It was just the way it was. By now, we had arrived at the airport, giving me the perfect excuse to end this conversation, but I silently promised myself to take Fulton's advice. As guilt struck as I thought about it, I vowed to take a break from my mom. I wasn't exactly sure how that would look or how long it would be, but I knew I'd figure it out as I needed to.

Later that night, once I was finally back in my apartment, I took the alone time to think, and I did something different. I took out a sheet of paper and wrote my mom a letter, telling her about my Christmas and wishing her well. Then before I lost my nerve, I sealed it and placed it on my desk so I could mail it the next day. I knew I couldn't disconnect totally from her, but I felt like a letter would be a nice stopgap for my physical presence until I had a real plan on how to proceed in our relationship.

Then I looked up counselors who were accepting new clients and found one who looked like a recent grad who had wide-open availability. She used online scheduling and since she was new to the practice, I was able to find an appointment time for this week. However, her availability wasn't the thing that was the most appealing to me. I loved the fact she had recently started her practice, so I knew she had never treated my mom. I felt like if I was going to do this break thing for real, and not just in vain, I needed to start fresh with everything.

Giggling seeped through my walls, cueing me that Becky had made it home, and I knew she was going to be up for a while, but I was drained. I plugged a bud in each ear, setting my playlist to start with Debussy, a composer I usually found anticlimactic, and I knew he could easily put me to sleep. Then I crawled into bed, texted Fulton, "Good night," and closed my eyes. I was nervous about the changes I was making, but I was also convinced that if I wanted new results, something had to change.

Chapter Fourteen

Arriving at the theatre the next morning before the sun was barely up, I took the early morning hours to catch up on my missed emails, and noticed an email from Bre's mom, relaying a roster of dance classes and their previous schedule. I let out an overwhelmed whistle when I realized the roster was printing out in pages, with no stop in sight. Now I regretted that I hadn't asked a little more about the logistics of their dance company before I volunteered to step up and assume full responsibility for their class space.

From the schedule, it looked like the company had two, and sometimes three classes, ongoing and overlapping in the afternoons, and a full preschool schedule in the mornings. I knew the mornings would be okay because we never had anything but play rehearsal before noon. However, I felt like pulling my hair out when I thought about the evening schedule because everyone needed to be out the door by six, at the latest, so they didn't interfere with our evening programming.

Making an executive decision to move all the high school ballet classes to early mornings before the school day, I nervously tugged at my ponytail when I pressed send on the email with the revised schedule. The girls would be upset that they had to dance before the sun was even up, but it was the only way this was going to work. Then rubbing my forehead from the strain I was feeling, I pushed my chair back and was startled to see Becky standing in my doorway. I sucked in my breath, then panted out, "You scared me half to death."

"Sorry."

"How long were you standing there?"

She casually strolled inside my office. A rustling sound from a brown bag she was holding caught my attention when she explained, "I just walked up."

"I bet you're looking for Wally," I said. "He wasn't here when I unlocked this morning, but it's still super early."

"No, I know he isn't here." She pointed to the couch. "Can I sit?"

"Sure." I reluctantly agreed, not because I didn't care to see her, but it was super odd for her to show up to my work when I could easily see her at home.

She sat on the sofa, resting her sack in the center of her lap, then pulled off her leather winter gloves, setting them neatly next to her.

"Do you have the day off?" I fished, trying not to sound like I didn't want her here.

"No, I've been coming in here in the mornings a couple days a week to help Wally out."

"You have?" My forehead scrunched because I knew this had to have started when I was in Montana, but I had only been gone a few days and she spoke like it was old news.

"Yeah, Wally was telling me how he missed doing more comedy shows, but he barely had the time to write any scripts since he's been managing everything, plus directing these shows. Comedy's his passion, so I offered to come in the mornings to help with some of the easy stuff so he can take some time to write."

"Oh." I let my voice slide over her comment as I was still perplexed at how the routine had changed so abruptly when I had only been gone a few days. "So, he's working on his comedy now?"

"Actually, no, he was supposed to, but he ended up getting sick last night. He has some respiratory virus thing, so he probably won't be in at all." She held her hand up in a confirming stop and said, "You don't have to worry, though. I'll take care of everything he was supposed to do."

"Okay . . ." I said, wondering why he never texted me to tell me he was going to be out for the day. Maybe sending Becky in his place was his new way of communicating with me. It felt odd, but I knew at this point I didn't have any say, so I chose not to dwell on it.

Her eyes gently latched onto mine, and she pulled her lips up in a non-energetic smile. "Did you have a nice time in Montana?"

"I did. It was nice to get away from work for a couple of days and be somewhere completely different."

"I'm glad."

I studied her sitting so casually on my sofa and decided that maybe she had just felt chatty since I had been gone, so I kept the conversation going, "What did you end up doing?"

"Wally and his folks came to my mom's for dinner."

I raised an eyebrow. "Really?" I wasn't sure why I was surprised because those two were already inseparable, but the noncommittal side of my brain sent an alarm out, wanting to caution Becky that it was way too soon in their relationship to be melding families.

She nodded with a coy smile on her face that made me think she was keeping something from me, but even in that, I could tell she was happy. "It was lovely." Was the only detail she expanded on.

"That's nice," I said with accidental sarcasm.

Becky lowered her brow. "What do you mean?"

"I said that sounds nice."

"Nah, you said it like you didn't really mean it."

"I do mean it," I defended, not wanting to get into any drama with her. She had her life, and I didn't care to meddle any more than what I was already being thrown into the middle of since she started dating my boss.

She jerked her head to the side, looking at me with a sideways glance. "It bothers you that Wally and I are seeing each other, doesn't it?"

Becky and I were never the friends to hide things from each other, but we were also never the type of friends who disclosed everything. We sort of hovered in middle ground where we knew some things were private. Feeling inundated with this information and now an accusation, I rubbed my forehead, trying to figure out how I felt about their relationship. Settling on some of the minor truths, after a short pause, I admitted, "It feels like you guys are moving really fast."

I was prepared for her to get defensive again, but instead, her smile reignited. "I know. We are."

"Doesn't it scare you?" I tried to conceal my own nausea over the idea of commitment.

"No, it doesn't. It feels *so* right. I know it's weird. We've only known each other for a few weeks, but the other day I was trying to remember what my life was like before we knew each other, and I honestly couldn't. Then I realized I didn't want to either." When she looked at me, her eyes sparkled, and I swore I could see pure puppy love pour out. "I feel like we were made for each other."

"I've never seen you like this." I still wanted to gag, but I didn't want to sound like I was a bad friend, so I dug deep and pulled my lips into a tiny grin.

"I've never felt like this." Her lashes batted like she was feeling all the feelings. It was obviously too late to talk any sense into her and I don't know how it happened, but she had fallen in love with my boss.

"Don't you think it's better to slow down and get to know each other a little better before you go all in?" I asked, thinking I would give it one more try to get her to see how irresponsible she was being.

Not wasting a second, she shook her head. "That's

just it. We do know each other. We talk for hours every day, and I feel like he knows me better than anyone ever has." The fact that it had been forever since I had been able to sleep without my earbuds reminded me that she was telling the truth. There were so many nights where I honestly didn't think either one of them slept because I swore I could hear her giggling through my wall *all night long*. She interrupted my thoughts by prompting me, "Don't you think it's amazing how we ended up dating best friends? I mean, we couldn't have planned it better. Like we can take vacations together, spend holidays together, attend our kids' birthday parties. It makes me so happy to think about all the cool things we can all do together."

"Kids," I choked. "Don't you think it's a little soon for you to think about kids?"

She shrugged, squaring her eyes plainly on mine. "Why not?"

"How long have you known Wally?" I asked, not because I'd forgotten, but I was seriously starting to think she had forgotten she had just met him.

She waved my question away by brushing her hand through the air. "Oh, Abs, don't be a pessimist. You know I've always been a hopeless romantic. All I ever wanted was to get married and have a bunch of kids."

"Since when?" My words came out through a snorted laugh as I didn't remember her talking about that stuff—ever. Tina, our other friend, had always been boy crazy and I had assumed she would be the one to go to school to get a misses degree, but Becky seemed to have more sense than that. Apparently, Becky was the type of girl who basically lost her whole common sense when she fell in love.

"Maybe not always," she relented, "but now that I have Wally, it's all I can think about."

I took a deep breath, letting it out slowly as this was a little too deep of a conversation for first thing Monday morning. I wasn't going to change her mind, but I still felt like she was being crazy, so I took one more chance. "I'm glad you're happy. Wally's a great guy. However, there's no rush. You guys can date for a while and figure things out." I knew I sounded like an old grandma, but Becky wasn't seeing any of the risks, and it was terrifying me.

"You know," she started, then echoed my deep sigh and said, "I know it's more common these days to date forever, wait until careers are established, the 401ks are funded, and do everything practical, but I don't want to be practical." She gazed above my head now like she was setting her sights on some imaginary stars and then dramatically she ended this declaration with, "I want to be in love and live in the moment. If people think it's too soon to feel this way, let them. I'm going to live my life my way."

"Okay . . ." was all I could say because we obviously had two very different ways of approaching a relationship. I let my eyes drift to the bag still resting in her lap. "So what's in the bag?"

"Oh." She sat up straight, her face instantly pinching into discomfort. "I forgot I brought you something."

"Me?"

"Don't get excited. It's nothing fancy." She opened the sack, pulling out a pint-sized carton of ice cream. Then her hand went back into the bag to pull out a second carton, and she reached across the room, handing it to me.

Reluctantly retrieving the ice cream while I checked my watch, I said, "It's like nine-thirty in the morning."

"I know." She handed me a plastic spoon while keeping her eyes low and said, "But trust me, you're going to need it."

I peeled off the lid. Fixated on my brown dessert, I asked, "So, what's really going on?" Feeling a knot build in my stomach, I waited.

Avoiding eye contact, she dove her spoon into the center of her pink-colored ice cream and then said, "So . . . I have something sort of crazy to tell you."

I could tell by her voice that crazy didn't mean anything good and the fact that she had brought ice cream at nine-thirty in the morning solidified that crazy actually meant something really bad. Thankful for the distraction, I copied her avoidance and dug into my own carton. "Okay," I squeaked out.

"You know how my mom is friends with your mom."

A cold chill went up my spine. *Yeah, this is going to be bad crazy, and I'm going to need ice cream.* Holding my breath, I dove my spoon into the middle of my carton. My head was immediately overloaded with all the embarrassing things that could possibly come out of Becky's mouth and I put my emotional shield up, waiting for Becky to say more.

The thing about Becky and me was that although we

were friends, our friendship had always been compli-
cated because our moms were friends and my mom
would tell her mom things. Becky always knew way too
much about my life for me to be comfortable with. She
was the one person—other than Fulton—who always
knew the truth. I hated it more than I appreciated it, but
it did cement a bond between us that I didn't have with
any of my other friends. My palms were a little sweaty
now as I fed myself my first bite and said, "Yeah."

"So, I told my mom that I was going to start helping
Wally out a couple mornings down here and she pointed
out that there would be a lack of office coverage at her
office." Her eyes were locked on her carton, and I knew
it wasn't because she loved ice cream that much, but it
was the gentle way she approached this issue, allowing
me a weird privacy so I wouldn't have to see her look at
me. She was committed to giving me my space. "So, my
mom," she continued, "hired your mom to work at her
office."

"How? She is going to go to jail," I blurted out.

"My mom talked to her lawyers, and they think
since there's a long-documented history of mental
health issues, they will be able to use that in her
defense. They said their main concern is that since your
dad has passed, she seems to lack an oversite and we
need to make sure she is getting the care she needs.
The lawyers think the state will step in and strip her of
all her rights, unless she is able to prove that she can
function on her own and that she has people assisting
her. My mom's hopeful that she can lean in with
support by offering her a part-time job, to show the

157

judge that she can function, and she has people looking out for her."

I blinked, then I blinked again. I still didn't have words, so I dug another huge hole in my ice cream, scooped it out, shoved it into my mouth, and waited for it to melt. It was perfect because I wanted to scream but I couldn't because my mouth was full. Becky was a genius when she brought ice cream! The amount of time it took for the ice cream to melt was enough for me to digest what she said, but I still had so many questions. "How is she going to work in the city? She—" I started to say she lived in Virginia but then I remembered she burned her house down and didn't have a place to live anymore, but even still New York was insanely expensive. I knew Becky's parents were beyond loaded, but they weren't going to pay her enough to afford rent on a part-time receptionist job.

"My mom's letting her rent a micro-studio unit in one of the buildings she owns in Brooklyn. It'll be a small commute but nothing uncommon."

My head was starting to spin from how ridiculous this was that my best friend was telling me my mom was moving to the city and got a job and *my* mom never bothered to tell me herself and now technically Becky was going to be my mom's boss! "When did all this happen?"

"It sort of all happened when you were gone." She played with her spoon by scraping it lightly over the top of the ice cream and I knew she was holding out something else.

"You can tell me."

"It's really not a big deal. I just thought you should know because I don't want to keep anything from you, but you know how I said that I had dinner at my mom's?"

"Yeah."

"Your mom was there," she said softly.

"You saw my mom and didn't say anything?"

For the first time since this conversation started, she lifted her eyes to mine. "I didn't know she was going to be there. Promise." Then perfectly on cue to give me my space, she lowered her eyes back to her ice cream. "My mom had insisted she come so she wasn't alone."

In the moment I was grateful for the friend that Becky was too me. As awkward as this was, she did everything she could to try to make it bearable. I put the lid back on my ice cream, because I had to be done talking about this. Then standing up, ready to leave this conversation behind me, I offered, "I can help you stock concessions since Wally's not coming in."

She also stood and perfectly picked up the new conversation. "I was able to reorganize the paper products in the cupboard the other day, so now there's a lot more room for extra supplies."

I actually smiled at how fast she transitioned from talking about my mom, and I didn't waste time leaving it behind either. "I hate the cupboard," I said. "It was like at the point where you pretty much had to open the door, toss whatever you needed to store in there as fast as you could, and then slam the door shut before everything cascaded out."

"I know! I couldn't take it either, so I stayed up until midnight the other night cleaning it."

"You did?" I quirked a brow because I didn't know she cared that much to give up her free time. By now we were behind the concession counter, and I walked to the cupboard to see for myself.

"Yeah, Wally was cleaning the auditorium, so I found my own project." She opened the door, beaming, and said, "Voila!"

"Looks great." I admired how she had even put labels on the shelves to mark where everything was supposed to go.

"Now if I can only stop myself from eating all the candy while I'm back here, then I'll be seriously happy." She smiled slyly as she reached under the counter and retrieved a box of chocolate-covered almonds. "I put everything on a tab, but then Wally rips it up so then there's no incentive for me not to eat it." She giggled as she ripped open the top of the box, and poured a couple out, offering me some.

Putting my hand out to cover her offerings, I refused. "No, seriously, I just pounded a pint of ice cream, and it isn't even noon. There's no way I can handle more sugar."

She shrugged, popping one into her mouth. "Suit yourself." Then she immediately set her eyes on the boxes of freight stacked on the back counter. I let out another sigh of relief because I knew she had already committed to forgetting about our talk and my secret was safe with her.

Chapter
Fifteen

Once I was finally able to leave the theatre for the day, I remembered I hadn't talked to Fulton since we had parted ways from our trip. I pulled out my phone, calling him while I walked. He promptly answered on the second ring. "Hey."

"Hey," I greeted him through the smile on my face.

"How are you?" he asked. This time I detected a raspiness in his voice.

"I'm walking home. Were you up all night studying again?"

"No." He cleared his throat. "I think I'm coming down with a cold."

"Wally was sick today too with some respiratory thing."

"That's probably what I'm getting. There are a lot of germs going around with the holidays."

"I suppose. Everyone gets together."

"Right."

I took a moment to tuck my long hair behind my ear, as the wind was starting to blow it in front of my face, both annoying me and making it difficult to see before offering, "Do you need me to bring you anything? Maybe some soup?"

"Nah, I wouldn't want to get you sick. And I'm not even hungry. Food sounds disgusting right now."

"That's too bad. Maybe all that traveling wore down your immune system."

"I'm guessing, but like I said, it's not anything terrible. I think if I can rest well tonight, I'll be back to normal by tomorrow." He cleared his throat again. Then added, "So you said Wally was gone. Was work pretty crazy?"

"No, not really because I guess Becky is working there now."

"What?" His voice seemed to slide up an octave at the end of his word.

"Yeah, she's helping out." I debated in my head if I wanted to continue this conversation, knowing where it was going to lead, or if I needed to find an excuse to hang up. Not wanting to have any secrets between us, I decided it was best to tell him the biggest news of my day. "So, yeah, Becky is going to work part time for Wally and then to cover the hours that she isn't at her mom's office, her mom hired my mom."

Just for fun, I counted the seconds it took for Fulton to respond. I figured I would get to about four or five, but he made it a solid eleven seconds before saying, "Really?"

"Yep. Apparently, her mom is stepping in with her big lawyers to try to get my mom back into a respectable place in society."

"What about the charges she was facing?"

"I don't know for sure if she was officially charged, but the way Becky was talking, she sounded like her mom's lawyers didn't think it was a big deal. I sort of learned a long time ago that when it comes to Becky's parents, things pretty much always work out the way they want them to." As I explained this to Fulton, I surprisingly felt a tiny bit of relief around the issue of my mom. Ever since my dad had passed, I had this giant boulder of responsibility weighing me down, and I never felt competent to handle any of it. Now that Becky's parents were assisting my mom, especially with her legal troubles, I felt like the boulder had shrunk a teeny bit.

"She still has to be punished, doesn't she?"

"I don't know. I didn't ask, but ever since I've known Becky, I know that whatever her parents want to happen, pretty much always happens. I wouldn't doubt it if they have half the judges in this town on their payroll."

"I didn't think her family was like that."

"I don't think it's anything illegal," I clarified. "Her parents do business with a lot of people. For example, I remember when the city was rezoning to try to free up space for more affordable houses, the city had decided to purchase an old utility building to remodel into a homeless shelter, but it was across the street from a couple of buildings her parents owned. Everything was set as the city had planned it for months, but her dad made one phone call and mysteriously the deal fell through."

"Really?"

"Yeah, stuff like that was always happening with them. I guess you can do that when you are billionaires."

"That's crazy because she seems so normal."

"She was spoiled like all of us who went to private school, but maybe it wasn't as bad as it could have been because she went to boarding school for most of her primary school years. I don't think she even understood herself who her parents were until she was well into high school."

"Hm—" Fulton broke his thought with a deep cough, making me wince.

"You sound terrible."

"Thanks," he said with laughter in his voice.

"You also sound tired."

"I am."

"Well, I'll let you go then, but call me if you need anything."

"I'll be fine. I just need to go to bed."

"Good night."

"Love you." Even though his voice was hoarse—the fact that we were now regularly saying I love you was a new thing to us—and it still gave me a trickle of goose-bumps, making my lips curl up.

"I love you too." When I said it, I felt brave like I had done something totally life-threatening like jumping out of an airplane even though the two things didn't have anything remotely in common. Normal people wouldn't be able to understand the fear behind it, but to me, saying I love you wasn't only about expressing my feelings. It opened me up to a whole realm of vulnerability that I wasn't even close to being comfortable with. Even though my feelings were real, it didn't change the fact that they still scared me to death. Fulton ended the call from his end, so I tucked my phone into my coat pocket, and headed home, feeling good about the day. Even though it hadn't been perfect, it had worked out.

Chapter Sixteen

As soon as I arrived at work the following morning, I was inundated with the first waves of the dancers. I hadn't exactly figured out the perfect space for their classes, so in the moment, I did damage control and said, "I'm working on a place for you to be able to have a barre, but I just got back from vacation, and my boss is out right now so I'm going to need a few more days to figure that out." A couple of the girls rolled their eyes, but most of them were graceful and took the news in stride.

This was the high school class, and I knew they'd be my toughest group. Most of the girls visually carried around a refined self-confidence that made me miss the diligence and routine of dancing. My morning to-do list quickly became a distant memory as I froze against the wall, watching them go through their warm-up stretches. There was a steady stream of girls arriving, and when I thought there was no way we could fit anyone else into the class, another girl would pass through the front door. It would be an understatement to say this was a tight squeeze, and I started to break a sweat.

The instructor—who looked like she was about my age—breezed through the front door, instantly commanding perfect classroom management. To deal with the limited space, she broke the girls into two groups, allowing one group to practice on the stage—which was also interesting and crowded because it was set for our play—and the other girls to remain in the lobby.

After the class, I was feeling a little embarrassed about my accommodations and I walked up to the instructor as she was slipping on her jacket. "I'm sorry for the tight squeeze," I said. "Everything was last-minute, and I had no idea your classes would be this big. Especially for the advanced ones."

"It's okay." Her perfect white teeth peeked out from a genuine smile. "I completely understand. We are all floundering right now with the studio being shut down so abruptly."

"I'm going to talk to my boss to see if there's a bigger space we can use."

She didn't waste a second letting me apologize further. "It's totally fine. Seriously, some of these girls need a reality check and the rest of them understand perfectly."

I chuckled, knowing I would have definitely been one of the girls who had needed a reality check when I was their age, and thinking back, a reality check had been the best thing that had ever happened to me. "Do you teach any of the other classes too?" I chatted to make small talk.

"I have a group of the preschoolers and then I come back for hip hop this afternoon."

"Nice," I said. "That keeps you busy."

"It does. Plus, I take classes at the beauty school in between so I feel like I am constantly running."

"I know the feeling."

About to excuse myself, she surprised me by asking, "You don't dance anymore?"

"Ah, no . . . I don't." I tilted my head toward her. "How'd you know I danced?"

"We were in the same ballet class." I racked my brain, but nothing came to mind. "Erica," she said, relieving me from my blank slate.

My mind rewound, remembering Erica very clearly, but she was slightly chubby and had lots of acne. I distinctly remembered being mean to her on more than one occasion. In fact, we had been somewhat rivals, always competing for the principal ballerina. The woman who stood in front of me now was slender, with perfect skin, and probably one of the prettiest smiles I had seen in a while. My cheeks grew warm. "I do remember you," I said, pausing to consider if I needed to apologize for my past rude behavior or if it was better to leave it unsaid to avoid further embarrassing us both. I decided on the latter, and offered the sincerest compliment I could, "You look great."

"Thank you." Her dark eyes lowered to the ground,

and I figured she was swallowing a few sharp words she had for me. She zipped up her coat, then looked back at me. "I need to run to class, but I'll be back in a couple of hours. It was great running into you again."

"You too." I smiled at her and watched her walk out the front door, just as Becky arrived. "Hey," I called out. "Is Wally still sick?"

She pulled one of the corners of her mouth into a patient grin. "I think he's a little better, and he did go to the walk-in clinic last night to get some stuff from the doctor, so he might be able to come in tomorrow once that kicks in."

"Shoooot." I let my disappointment drown out in how long I stretched out my Os.

Her face chippered as she looked up a me. "Oh, I'll be here all day to help out again."

"I wasn't too worried about coverage, but I wanted to ask Wally something."

"Well, you can ask me. I'll try to help."

I resisted laughing at the ridiculous way that Becky was acting like my supervisor just because she's been dating my boss for a few weeks. "Maybe you can . . ." I didn't see how she would know anything more than I did, but I could also see that she was genuinely trying to help, so I went ahead, explaining, "I didn't know what I was getting into when I agreed to host these dance classes. They are a lot bigger than I thought they would be. When I had visualized hosting the classes, I sort of saw them practicing on the stage, but I totally over-looked the fact that the stage is still set for our play and that takes up most of the open space. So, I had an embarrassing morning because I didn't have a plan. I let them spread out over the lobby and auditorium, but it's not going to work well long term because they are going to need one large space. I was wondering if Wally knew of a better way that we could fit everybody in."

Her lips pursed out, then she said, "Ah, you know there is an area in the basement that could be cleared out if we could move some shelves and boxes."

"I didn't even know we had a basement," I replied, my brows knitted together. "How'd you know there was a basement?"

She gave me a scrunchy-nose grin and said, "I was down there looking for the cats when they got out."

"Oh no." I covered my mouth, sucking in a long breath before squeaking out, "I forgot about that. How bad was it?"

"Not too bad. One of the stacks of cages fell over, and then when the cages landed on their sides, a few of the doors unlatched. We joked it was a planned escape because we still don't know how the cages fell over, but there was a lot of commotion going on backstage with all the actors and dancers, so who knows."

I winced through my narrowed eyes. "Was Wally mad?"

"No, because we adopted out over twenty cats. Even the humane society was here, interviewing Wally, and the publicity from that article sold out the rest of our shows, so he thought that was cool."

"That is good news." My eyes lingered on her while I felt a decompression in my chest.

"Plus, it feels good to do something good for the

community and this play has made so much money, I think we could have elephants roaming around back here, and he'd put up with it."

I giggled when I thought about the mess that a fugitive elephant would create. "It's like *Phantom of the Opera* but it's an Elephant that lurks in the shadows. Oh, man," I said, teasingly, sounding bummed, "That could totally be our next production if Wally hadn't banned live animals."

"Yeah, as happy as he is with how this play has turned out, it's been too much of a logistics crunch to make sure the cats get out for exercise, are fed, and keeping everything clean. Actually" —she leaned closer to me and continued in a lowered voice— "we're still missing one cat so keep your eyes open for it."

"Oh, really? Hmm," I thought out loud, "I haven't seen anything."

"I feel awful that we lost him, but hopefully he ends up in a better place." Then Becky's eyes swept the lobby in front of us. "So, you want an open place where all the dancers have room to fit. I'd start with the basement because it's too cold to be on the roof this time of year."

"What were you doing on the roof?" I asked in disbelief because I also hadn't been up there.

She pushed her lips a little pouty in my direction before saying very firmly, "Cat stuff."

I giggled when I pictured Becky scaling the roof with a giant net. Of course, my imagination had her wearing an all-black jumpsuit, and goggles, which was totally out of character for her because she wasn't much of a person for hands-on work. "Sorry," I apologized again. Then I started thinking about how Becky and I have had our shares of ups and downs in our friendship, but I was grateful for where we were now, even though the whole dating-my-boss thing was beyond weird, so I took a moment and said, "I have to admit, at first when I had learned that you and Wally were like a thing, it was hard and it's still weird for me sometimes, but I really appreciate your friendship."

"Ah, me too." She got her sappy-eyed I'm gonna-hug-you look on her face and leaned in for a side hug. "I missed you so much when we weren't talking, and it's been so great being friends again."

I waited until she was done squeezing me. "Okay, can you show me where the basement is?"

"Sure." Her smile grew wide on her face. "Just let me grab my set of keys."

"Of course you have your own set of keys." I followed her to the back office. "Why wouldn't you?" Then I chuckled to myself about how weird this was, but in the strangest of ways, I now was starting to love it and didn't want to change it.

Chapter Seventeen

Becky and I heaved all the boxes in the basement like they were full of ticking time bombs until we had everything moved out of the way. I was prepared—but out of breath—to receive the preschool class when the next dancers came running through the doors. Panting, I propped the basement door wide-open with my foot, and supervised the girls' parade down the stairs.

"Oh, they are so cute! Look at them—like tiny princesses," Becky squealed, covering her mouth as the tutu-wearing tots ran past her. "I can't wait to have a little girl."

I choked a little, but then covered my mouth and coughed an extra time to make it look like it wasn't in reaction to her comment. Then I nonchalantly said, "They are cute, but we def have a while before we have to worry about having our own, right?"

"I don't want to wait. They are too precious. I want a whole minivan full of babies."

I bit my tongue, thinking Wally had his hands *full* with her. Before I could reply, a loud cry came from the bottom of the steps. I ran down to find one of the girls holding her nose—a spring of fresh blood was flowing out from the bottom of her hand. "Oh, honey, come here." I reached out to steer her back up the stairs. "We need to get some tissue from the bathroom."

Then Becky came flying down the stairs with a stack of napkins from the concession stand, handing them to me. "Here."

"Thanks." I grabbed the napkins and wrapped them on the girl's nose, taking a second to check if there was anything abnormal about the bleed. "You're going to be fine," I reassured her. Then I asked, "What happened?"

"I was spinning, and I tripped and landed on Olivia's elbow."

"Yep, that happens. I've had a few elbows in my nose too." I held the napkin on her nose for a minute longer, then checked it but it was mostly dried up. "I think you're done bleeding, but let's go to the bathroom anyway so we can wash up." She followed me up and at the top of the stairs, we met Erica, who had arrived to teach the class.

"What happened?" she asked when she saw me steering the girl with my hand still attached to her nose.

"Just an elbow," I said. "She's fine. We are going to wash."

"Okay, good." She looked behind her at the mostly empty lobby. "I was confused about where everybody was when I walked in, but I saw the open door. Are we down here now?"

"Yeah, I'm sorry," I called back as I continued to pace toward the bathroom. "It was a last-minute decision because you'll have more room down there. I should have sent a text. Sorry."

"It's cool," she called back as she started to head down the stairs. "I'll send a text now to the parents who are still on their way."

"Thanks," I called back and had no idea if she had heard me because I was going through the bathroom door now. Letting out a tired sign, I resigned myself to the fact that it was way more work to host these dancers than I had thought it was going to be. I hadn't had any time to do any of my other duties, but I managed to get the girl cleaned up and back in class. Then I ended up staying for the rest of the class to make sure she didn't get bumped again. When I finally had the place cleared out, I knew I was going to have to work late tonight—and probably every night—because there was no way I was going to get anything done when I had dancers here. They required an extra set of eyes, especially the younger dancers, and I didn't want anything bad to happen that would reflect on Wally.

I pulled out my phone to text Fulton that I was going to work late but saw a missed call from my aunt Kim. I was about to press send on her name to call her back, but an incoming call from Fulton flashed on my screen. I accepted it and said, "Hi, how are you?"

"Still sick." I didn't even need to hear the words because his voice was so weak, it sounded transparent.

177

"You don't sound well at all." I headed back to my office to talk. "Have you gone to the doctor?"

"That's actually why I'm calling. I went to the student wellness center to see a PA, but she wanted me to get a chest X-ray, so I took a cab to the hospital. Now I'm here in the waiting room, but I discovered I don't have my insurance card because my mom had sent me a new one and I didn't put it in my wallet yet. I don't want to leave because I'll have to go to the end of the waiting list again and the wait is crazy long already. I tried calling my roommate, but he didn't answer. I hate to ask, but is there anyway you'd have time to run to campus and get my card?"

I checked the clock on my computer, calculating what time I would get there. "You really think your wait is going to be that long?"

"All the chairs are full, and I've only seen one person called back since I got here almost thirty minutes ago."

"Okay," I agreed, immediately reached for my coat and purse, and headed back out to find Becky. "I'll have to see if Becky can cover for me, because Wally's still out sick too, but I'm sure she will."

"Thanks."

"No problem."

"Do you need anything else while I'm at your place?"

"I don't think so. My insurance card should be sitting right on my desk. I'll keep trying to get ahold of my roommate, but if I can't, I'll call the RA to let you in."

My lips straightened. Not that he was allowed to

copy the dorm keys to give out to people, but it seemed like such a contrast that Fulton and I had been seriously dating for almost a year, and I still needed permission into his residence when Becky had a full set of janitorial keys to Wally's business after only a few weeks. "Okay, I'll call if I can't get in," I said. "If I don't call, I'll just see you later."

"Thanks."

"No prob."

"Love you."

"Love you too." I buzzed out the side stage door toward the back office to look for Becky, but I ended up finding her in the ticket office, talking on the phone, punching in numbers into the computer. As soon as she saw me, she placed the caller on hold, put the phone to her chest, and asked, "What's wrong?"

"Fulton's at the doctor and forgot his insurance card. He wants me to get it but it's going to take the rest of the afternoon. I hate to ask, but can you cover the matinee shift by yourself and also my dance classes tonight until I can make it back?"

"Sure." She waved me out the door. "Go ahead. I'll be here anyway."

"Are you sure?" I wondered how she knew how to do everything, but at the same time I was ecstatic that she did.

"I got it covered. Go to Fulton."

"Thanks." I waved bye but then bolted for the front door, breathing a little sigh of relief that she was so willing to help out. That part was easy at least. Now, I was going to have to find a way to bust into Fulton's dorm. I checked the train schedule on my phone, while I ran to Penn Station. Luckily, I hit the train station at the perfect time and I was able to grab an eastbound train with no time to spare. I slumped down into my seat, letting my body acknowledge that this was the first time I had sat down all day. Before I knew it, I had nodded off, taking a little snooze, making it feel like we took the shortcut to campus. Lucky for me, the train stopped right on campus, so I didn't have to worry about finding it. I'd been here before, but it had been a while and only once because it was such a trek, Fulton always visited me in the city because there was more to do.

Fulton's RA was waiting for me by the door when I tried to enter. "Wow, that's pretty efficient," I said as he let me inside the dorm hall.

"I was making my rounds and figured you'd be on this train." He headed down the hall, I followed in tow, making small talk, and his RA said, "Fulton's been pretty sick. Glad he went to the doctor."

"Yeah, me too. Thanks for helping me out."

"You're welcome." He stopped at Fulton's door and unlocked it, pushing it open. "Just lock it when you come back out."

"Thanks," I said and entered his room, heading straight to his desk. Taking a second to survey the top, I saw what looked like a stack of veterinary program brochures. I couldn't help but pick them up to browse. Right on top were the programs in New York. I flipped through the first brochure, excited to see all the fun stuff he'd be learning. All the students looked so professional with their white lab coats, and I easily pictured Fulton wearing one, and instantly had a proud girlfriend moment. Then my jaw fell open because I caught sight of the cost. Fifty grand a year just for tuition! I had no idea it was *that* expensive. After four years, he'd have a mortgage payment. Then I noticed a slip of notebook paper tucked inside and it had Fulton's handwriting on it. He had written out the math calculation, adding up the tuition with interest, compounding it for thirty years, and I gasped when I saw the total was over seven hundred thousand dollars! I had no idea interest would more than triple the borrowed amount!

I frantically flipped through the rest of the brochures from the other programs in New York. Most were around that same price. *At least he'll have a good paying job when he gets done,* I told myself. At the end of the stack was a folded letter with a recognizable University of Florida letterhead. It was his early acceptance letter from there, offering him a paid teaching assistantship. I placed the letter next to the stack of brochures from the New York programs, digesting the differences. One path was fully paid, and other path may present a more prestigious schools (that had been a point I had heard Fulton make to his mom) but would easily end up with hundreds of thousands in debt, something he had told me, but I knew I hadn't really understood it at the time.

When I looked at the schools side by side like this, there was a hollow in my heart because it was obvious which was the better option for him. Linda's words warning him of not having regrets rang in my ear. Fulton was financing this on his own and I knew I didn't want him to have a huge financial burden after he got done with vet school just because he didn't want to leave me.

My eyes paced his letter one more time, noting it hadn't been signed. I knew the reason he hadn't signed and returned it was because of me not wanting to move too. I didn't want to be a regret, I told myself as I restacked the papers the way I had found them. Remembering Fulton was waiting, I quickly located his insurance card. Then I spun on my heel, heading to the hospital, knowing exactly what I was going to do—insist Fulton take this assistantship. It was going to suck for me, but it was truly the best option for him.

Unfortunately, when I got to the hospital, they didn't let me past the front desk, so I wasn't able to talk to Fulton, but I left his card for him. Bummed I came all this way and didn't actually get to see him, I texted him, but didn't get a reply back. Assuming he was in with the doctor, I headed back to work to relieve Becky and unfortunately I didn't make it back in time for my dance classes. Everyone had all cleared out and the door was open receiving people for our night play. I weaved through people, on the look-out for Becky, passing the ticket counter and the concessions stand. I finally found her, ushering people to their seats in the auditorium with a smirk on her face. "Is there anything you haven't trained to do?" I asked when I walked up to her.

"I didn't train for any of it." She laughed. "It's been pretty much me doing what needs to be done."

"You are doing a great job," I complimented her and then asked, "How did dance class go?"

"Good." She headed back up the aisle toward the

door to receive more people. "Actually, Wally's dad came down for a couple of hours to grab the deposit, so he gave me a lunch break."

I felt my eyebrows lift and a seed of anxiety budded in my gut. "His dad came when all the girls were here?"

"Yeah." A lady walked up to Becky, and I waited while Becky checked her ticket, and then instructed her to go to the other side.

"Did he seem upset by the chaos?" I pressed, still feeling the need to wince.

"He seemed confused and didn't like the idea of the girls being downstairs. He thought it was probably some sort of code violation, but I explained that we were figuring things out and since Wally wasn't here, we just did that for the day."

"Then what'd he say?"

"Nothing really."

"As long as I didn't get Wally in trouble," I worried out loud.

"Nah, Henry's got a weakness for cute girls in trouble, so he won't care."

"Well, I haven't done an ounce of my regular work today," I admitted, feeling defeated, "but I can help you with this and then if you want to go home, I can stay for the show to lock up."

She immediately shook her head. "No, I told Wally I'd make sure everything was taken care of, so I'll be here, but if you want to go home, you can. I know you have dancers here at six and I'm actually not going to be able to come here tomorrow 'cause . . ." Her voice trailed off, but her eyes got wide.

"Why?" I asked, feeling a little suspicious.

She gritted her teeth in warning before saying, "Your mom is starting, so I need to be there—at least in the morning anyway—to train her. I mean, I know she won't need much training, but I have to make sure she can set up her computer profile and stuff."

"That's not going to be awkward," I said sarcastically.

"It won't be," she assured me. "It's fine. I'm not going to work there on the days she is there, so I won't see her much, but if you ever want to stop over there to see her, you're more than welcome—"

"I'm fine," I cut in. "I think if she wants to see me, she can come here. I'm sort of over running after her."

Becky's eyes traced my face, and I could tell she was biting her tongue. After a short pause, she said, "I understand."

"Okay, I'll see you at home then."

"Yep. Go ahead and go," she said, and so I did.

But as tired as I was, my insomnia kicked in right when I got into bed, so I texted Fulton.

Me: *Are you awake?*

Fulton: *Yeah.*

Me: *Can you talk?*

A second later my phone lit up with his name. I clicked on accept and said, "Hey."

"Hey," his gruff-sick voice replied.

"How are you feeling?"

"Awful."

"What did the doctor say?"

"I'm getting pneumonia, so he gave me some stuff,

184

but I guess we caught it in the early stages which I'm glad because I wouldn't want this in the later stage."

My mind flashed back to the only other time I had seen someone with pneumonia—when my dad passed away, and I was instantly filled with relief that Fulton had made it to the doctor and I was glad I had helped him. "Good thing you went in today."

"Yeah, I was getting nervous because I'd been missing classes and I don't want to get behind."

I washed the dryness of my lips away with my tongue before I bravely said, "I was thinking about your school today."

"Yeah?"

Knowing he was sick and exhausted, and this wasn't the best timing, I also knew it was going to gnaw at me until I addressed what I had seen today. Since we had a pattern of always having terrible timing for everything, I decided to stick with the pattern. "Actually, when I was in your dorm, I saw your vet program brochures and I looked through them because I wanted to see what it was all about . . ."

"Yeah?"

"It's pretty expensive, isn't it?"

"Yep."

"Do you think you can get an assistantship to one of the programs in-state?"

"It's hard to say for sure, but I doubt it, because they only usually have one or two slots and a lot of times it's who you know, and I don't really know anyone."

"Hmm."

"Why do you ask?"

"I know you told me before that it was so expensive, but I think it didn't register until I saw the breakdown of how you wrote everything out."

"Yeah, it's crazy expensive, but it'll be worth it. At least I don't have any debt from undergrad since my parents funded it."

"That is a nice benefit." I was getting a weird feeling in my gut, like the stillness you feel as you inch up a wooden roller-coaster, right before you get to the top it comes to almost a halt and your stomach drops because you know in the next second, the speed will unleash, and you will go death spiraling down. I closed my eyes, blurting out, "I want you to accept the Florida program. I know the only reason you haven't accepted that offer is because of me. But it's just too expensive not to accept an opportunity like that and I don't think I could live with myself if I knew you gave it up to stay close to me."

"I think you're rushing it a little. I don't even know what other programs I'll get accepted—"

"No, I'm not," I spoke over him. "You know what a good deal that is. It's a great program. The schools here are so expensive. Think for a minute about how much money you'll have to pay back. It will take half your life. We did the long-distance thing before, and I know we'll be fine."

"Is that how you really feel or are you just saying that because you feel guilty now that you saw the price tag?" His voice was so soft, and I could tell it wasn't just from him being sick. This was obviously a hard conversation for him too.

"It is how I feel, and I do feel guilty," I admitted.

"But when I think about it, it feels like a gift from my dad. I don't understand it yet and it's not how I would have preferred it to be, but I have to believe since he had his hand in it, it'll work out."

"I can see that too," Fulton said, and I heard him take a loud breath. "I tried to turn it down so many times already, but every time I sat down to fill out the papers to decline it, I would remember your dad made this happen for me . . . but also for us."

"So . . . can you please sign your letter and send it back?"

"I can. I still would like to wait to see what other programs I get into before I return it, but I know I need to let them know."

"And you can always change your mind if a better offer comes in, but I wouldn't want you to pass this one up."

"That's true . . ."

"So, you'll sign it and send it back as soon as you are feeling better?"

"I will." His promise hung in the air, and I knew he was resisting the building anxiety over the impending change.

"Good. And we don't need to worry about anything else because it'll be fine," I said more to reassure myself, because as much as I was convinced that this was the best thing for him, I also knew it would feel like a long four years being so far away. We ended our call, and I finally felt like my day was complete, so I closed my eyes and went to sleep, so I could get up in the morning to go to work and do my day all over again.

As the average working-days blurred together turning into weeks, I was waiting for a release of stress, but it seemed like my workload only doubled again. Now I had to set my sights on the next play: writing, designing costumes, and training dancers—all while still coordinating dance classes. I eagerly looked forward to spring when the dance classes would be wrapped up, and I could be fully relieved from that commitment, but true to the fashion of my life, things didn't really go the way I had planned them.

Chapter Eighteen

On one of the first warm spring days, Fulton and I anxiously waited in line for our cherished pork on a stick. We had taken a sabbatical from it while the weather was cold, but today we were back in line and we invited Wally and Becky to join us. Wally made sure to make fun of us, but quickly muted when he got his first taste. "This is delicious." His lips noisily smacked down the sticky flavor.

Fulton and I exchanged knowing looks, but we didn't stall to taste our lunches either. After a couple bites, Fulton reached into his pocket, pulled out two letters and handed them to me.

"What is it?" I asked, taking them both into my free hand.

"I got into a program in New Jersey and Massachusetts. Just thought it was cool."

"That's awesome!" I said, browsing the letters.

"No assistantship offers though. So, I'm relieved I accepted Florida when I did."

"Just wait, because you might still get something in state."

"I would think if it was going to be good news, they'd have notified me already."

"You're just nervous."

I kept my voice smooth to try to calm his nerves, but then I felt my eyes widen when I saw Fulton start to motion down the street. "Who's that waving at you?"

Shielding my eyes from the sun, I tried to focus and saw a middle-aged woman eagerly waving at me. It wasn't until she got closer that I was able to recognize her. "That's Bre's mom." I said in a hushed voice to Fulton and then I held my pork out to him. "Can you hold onto this? It looks like she wants to talk, and I can't feel professional while holding a stick of pork." He laughed, took the stick, and I stood up and waved back at her.

"I'm so glad I caught you," she said, sounding like she had run several blocks before she was finally able to halt her steps right in front of me. "I was having lunch down the street with a friend and was hoping you'd be around."

Taking a step closer to her, I tilted my head back to look at her and asked, "Sure, what's up?"

"I wanted to thank you for all your hard work with the girls." She leaned in a little closer and added, "I know it was a lot of work to take all these classes on at the last minute, but they love seeing you every day. Bre

190

can't ever say enough nice things about you. You really did save her year. Thank you."

"Ah, you're welcome." My smile grew from her praise. "It's been a lot of work, but I'm glad I was able to help."

"Well, as you know Bre's graduating this year, but some of the other parents are starting to make plans for next year, and they asked me if I knew what your plans were."

My face stiffened, now confused. "I wasn't planning anything for next year. I had assumed we'd be wrapped up in a month or two, and then the girls could find new companies over the summer."

"That's just it." She kept her eyes secured on me. "They don't want to find new companies. They love seeing you and most of these girls have danced together for years, if not a full decade. They want to stay together."

"That's sweet of you to say, but I don't see how I could impose on Wally any longer." I motioned to Wally, but then quickly regretted that move because he was woofing down his pork, not looking the least bit professional. So, in order to divert her attention away from him, I quickly said, "He's been a great sport having the classes here, but it really wasn't a good setup."

"Really? You don't think you can do it next year?" she echoed, her voice dropped at the end.

I shrugged, feeling the burden of an impossible situation. "I don't see how and it's not even fair because they need an appropriate dance studio. They missed out on being able to practice a lot of fun choreography because they didn't have the space to do it. Erica was amazing with finding ways to make it work, but I think she'd probably quit if she had to do this again."

"What if we found a better space for you to rent? Would you be interested in coordinating everything then?"

I let my mind process the request, but instantly saw a roadblock in my schedule. "There's no way. The class schedule is so sporadic and the only way it worked now was because I was already here all day because of my job. I could never commute back and forth to another space." I lowered my voice to a whisper and added, "Plus, since the girls were here, my boss was getting paid for the rental space, so he didn't mind if the classes took some of my time, but if I have to leave the building, and he's not getting paid for the space, I don't think he'll be so flexible."

"That's such a shame." The corners of her mouth drooped down when she added, "The girls are going to be so disappointed."

"Trust me, I'm beyond flattered," I said, "but they'll all adjust fine. There're so many phenomenal dance companies in the city. Plus, sometimes there's an advantage to finding a new instructor to train under because you learn different things from each one."

"That's true . . ." Her tone lifted, but her lips still hung a little at the edges. Then she placed a hand on my arm. "Well, I won't keep you any longer. It looks like you are on your lunch, but I'll let the other moms know that you officially made up your mind not to continue to coordinate the classes here."

"Thanks for doing that. Like I said, I didn't even realize they were thinking this was an option."

"Have a nice day," she said and walked away.

I turned back to my friends, grabbed my pork from Fulton, and commented, "That was interesting."

I wasn't going to give it another thought, but Wally spoke up, "I feel like you used me as an excuse."

"Why?"

"You basically said I was tolerating you, but that's not true. I enjoyed having the classes and I made a lot of extra money from the rent."

"You did," I agreed. "But you wouldn't want to continue at this pace though, would you?"

He shrugged, tipping his head toward me. "It's up to you."

"I'm exhausted," I defended. "Plus, I haven't had any time to work on my dance clothing line and I've already put money into it that I still need to try to get back and I actually *miss* it."

"I know you've been stretched," Fulton chimed in, "but I'm actually surprised you didn't think more about the offer because I thought you'd enjoy being around dance again."

"I do," I said slowly, "but it's different because I don't have any of the creative involvement with it right now. The instructors do all that, and I basically got stuck coordinating all the boring stuff."

"I see," Fulton said, but then inclined his chin and added, "What if you could be more involved with the creative stuff?"

"Like how?"

"Well, like you said, you are basically a coordinator right now, doing the minimum amount of stuff that needed to be done in the absence of the director, but you could totally build your own dance studio so you would be able to have more involvement with all the creative stuff. You already have dancers waiting for enrollment. I don't think it gets any easier than this."

"I can see what you're saying, but I don't think it's that simple."

"Why not?" Fulton questioned. His hazel eyes took a playful gleam like he was putting me on a dare.

"For one, again we are back to the space issue and for two, I don't have money to seed a business like that right now. Rent in the city alone is tens of thousands a month. I can't do it."

Fulton let out a sigh, like he was willing to concede on his dare. "Yeah, I guess that makes sense. Opportunity usually comes down to money."

"Yep," I agreed and had nothing else to add. My situation seemed to parallel Fulton's journey with veterinary school because both our dilemmas had two clear paths: one path where all dreams came true, but we couldn't afford it. The other path was the reality where we'd have to learn to settle.

But Fulton was more of an optimist than I was and he enjoyed each passing week because they would bring more acceptance letters, and so far, he had gotten accepted into every program he had heard back from. You would think it would become old news, but each new letter brought another wave of excitement for Fulton. By the end of the month, he had heard back from all of the out-of-state schools, but still nothing from an in-state program.

On our last week of dance classes, I was feeling sentimental and hired a photographer for class pictures. Matching my dad's marketing style, I took advantage of a marketing opportunity by bringing matching leg warmers from my dance clothing line for the preschoolers to wear for pictures. It turned out to be a pretty slick move because most of the mom's ended up purchasing the leg warmers because the girls didn't want to give them back, so I ended up making quite a few sales, making me excited to re-invest that money back into my clothing line. Then I was sitting on the floor, finishing folding the returned pairs, when Fulton walked through the front door.

I furrowed my brow. "Did your classes get canceled this morning?"

"One did so I had enough time to run in for a fast pork on a stick." He reached into the front pocket of his jacket and pulled out something—another letter—and handed it to me.

"Where is this one from?" I opened it, but when I saw the letterhead, I jumped off the floor. "What!" I squealed. "Why didn't you tell me right away? That's amazing. Congrats!" I jumped forward and gave him a huge hug, spinning him around in the process.

He stubbled backward to catch his balance and chuckled when he said, "I didn't know you'd be that excited."

"It's *Cornell*! And it's in STATE." A tightness in my chest that I didn't even know I had been holding onto released, knowing he had finally got accepted into an in-state school, but it only lasted a second when my heart was reminded that even though he got accepted, he wouldn't be able to take it.

"It's pretty surreal. That was my top choice." He took the letter back from me, folded it, and shoved it back in his pocket. "No scholarship, so I guess the plan hasn't changed."

I didn't know why it stung so bad this morning, because Florida had been the plan for weeks now, but up until now, he hadn't had an offer from a New York school. Now, he was holding his first choice in-state school in his hands, and he looked so proud. I had to imagine that it stung to know he did everything he could over the last four years to get accepted but now, it didn't matter. I hung onto his arm and looked up at him. "Do you want to go even a little bit?"

"Of course. Who wouldn't want to go to Cornell? But it's also the most expensive program I've been accepted into, and they didn't offer me any scholarship, so it doesn't seem logical."

"You'd be pretty marketable once you got that degree though."

He flashed his easy grin at me. "Sometimes I think you missed your true calling and should have followed your dad into marketing. I think you secretly love it."

Laughing, I quickly denied it. "No, it's not a calling at all, but it was my brainwashing for years. Hard to break the habit."

Fulton's eyes floated above my head as he scanned the room. "Are you working by yourself?"

"I didn't think so, but I don't know where Wally is. Becky had an open house this morning. However, I thought I saw Henry in the office when I came here, but that might have been a dream, because I haven't seen him since."

"That's too bad because I was wondering if you could take a break to grab a stick."

I straightened my lips into a disappointed line. "I shouldn't leave since I'm the only one here, but you can go ahead—" I stopped talking because I saw both Becky and Wally come flying through the front door together, with matching smiles so large they could compete with Alice's Cheshire Cat. "What have you two been up to?" I asked, suspiciously.

Becky waved at me urgently. "Abs! You *have* to come with us!" I was about to ask why when I saw Henry and Becky's mom both walk in the door with equally large grins, adding to the mystery of their recent absence.

Henry looked at me and winked. "You're gonna love it."

A little delayed in my thought processing, I began to understand that they had all been gone *together*, which piqued my interest even more. "What's going on?"

"Just come with us," Becky urged.

I made a squeamish smile when I asked, "Where are we going?"

"Not far. Just come with." She was seriously jumping up and down, like a five-year-old who believed Santa was waiting outside with his sleigh.

"Okay. Okay." I gave in and followed them all out the door. They all had these crazy smiles on their faces.

Even Fulton's smile stretched wide across his face. When I finally looked at him, I couldn't help but ask, "Do you know what's going on?"

"No. I wish I did."

We walked outside and took a few steps down the street, when Becky immediately turned, entering the building next door. I had never been inside that building because it looked like it was another average souvenir shop, and I didn't have any use for trinkets. Instead of going into the retail shop, though, Becky opened a side door that headed up a staircase to the top floor. When we got to the top, her mom stepped in front, with a key, unlocking the door, revealing a short hallway with a door on each end.

Before I could ask any questions, Becky's mom explained, "There used to be two apartments on this floor but a few years ago the owner remodeled one of the units on this side for commercial use, but lately he's had a hard time keeping tenants. The one he had moved out, and he got another one and they were only here a short while too. Then the renters he had in the apartment broke their contract and left, citing a bunch of weird stuff. They said it was haunted. He decided because the market is so strong to sell these units and contacted me to see if I could list this whole floor together. I brought Becky and Wally down here because I knew they were looking for a closer place for Wally to stay so he wouldn't have the commute, and with the location so ideal, I knew it had to be perfect."

I felt my head jolt back while my eyes locked on Becky. "You guys are looking for an apartment?"

"I started to look for a place closer to the theatre," Wally said. "The commute out to Long Island is too long for my hours and as you know, half the time I crash in my office." Then he looked at his dad and said, "Plus, it's time I move out of my parents' house, and I made extra money with all the dance rent that I can afford it now."

Becky chimed in, "So he asked me if my mom had any listings, but when Wally and I started talking about it, we realized that we both pretty much saw us being together, so it made sense for us to look together."

"So, you guys bought an apartment?" I connected the dots.

"We did!" Becky squealed. "It needs renovating because guess what the ghost was!"

"Um, there was a real ghost?"

"It was the cat we lost!" Becky exclaimed. "I have no idea how he made it over here, but he was mostly living in the vents, causing a lot of weird noises, but at the same time, he made a lot of little messes, but that's okay because we figured it would be another six months or so before we get married, so we have time to get it fixed up." My head was spinning, from the cat to their apartment, to their ideas of marriage. Before I could congratulate them, Becky continued, "But that's not the coolest part!"

"It's not?" I asked, sort of sarcastically. "I can't see how it gets better than this."

"We initially had planned on renting, but we talked to Henry about it, and he agreed he'd purchase the apartment."

"Oh," I said, not understanding how this was at all that exciting for me.

"Then when we brought him down here to look at the apartment, he couldn't get over how nice of a space it was, but he also worried about what would happen when the commercial space was sold because we'd be living right there, and he wanted to make sure we wouldn't have to combat a bunch of noise. Then we started tossing around ideas and he decided to purchase both spaces."

"Hm," I said, still following their story.

"You have to see it!" Becky grabbed my hand, yanked me down the hall and opened the door, revealing the wide commercial suite, pretty plain looking but it had solid wood floors. "Isn't it perfect for your dance studio?"

I did a double take at her. "What?"

"You can rent it for deed from Henry and use it as your dance studio!" Becky was squeezing my hands and jumping up in down, practically shouting in my face.

I winced at her volume level. "What are you talking about?"

"Remember when we were eating outside, and I overheard Bre's mom ask you to continue to coordinate the girls' dance classes? You *said* you enjoyed it, but the space didn't work out. This is perfect because you don't have a commute. You're right next door!"

My eyes bounced from Becky to Henry to Wally. Then I looked at Fulton, who grinned back at me, but he looked as surprised as I felt. "I can't believe you didn't ask me before you did this."

"Because I knew you'd insist on us not doing it," Becky said.

Then Wally said, "I know you think I didn't like the dancers at the theatre, but I actually think it's an amazing partnership because we have a steady stream of performers for our plays or other shows, and they have a regular place to perform. However, I agree that we need to transition the girls to a better space, and this is perfect."

Henry interjected, "There isn't any pressure. I loved the space. It's prime real estate and since the rumor was that it was haunted, I got it for a bargain. I can easily find a renter if you decide it's not something you want to take on, or we may just use it for play rehearsals, so we have more flexibility too." He waved a hand toward the space. "There are so many options."

I chewed my lip, trying to find an excuse, or at least a polite way to say no, but I didn't want to say no because Becky was right. It was literally next door to the theatre so I could easily coordinate classes and help the instructors as needed. There really couldn't be a more perfect setup. I looked at Henry and confirmed, "I don't need any down payment and I can rent it from you and pay monthly?"

He gave a warm smile, like I was joining a team. "Yes."

Then I looked at Wally. "And you don't have an issue if I'm over here doing stuff during my workday?"

"I don't." He scratched the back of his head, then added. "You always gave me more than enough hours.

I've never felt like you weren't giving the theatre enough."

Becky took my hand again and squeezed it. "So. You'll do it?"

My eyes locked back on Fulton's, needing a sign that I wasn't about to make a terrible decision, but he was grinning and gave me a nod. Then before I lost my nerve, I looked back at Henry and said, "Deal. Let's do it."

Becky cheered, like I scored the winning touchdown, which made us all laugh. I shook my head, not knowing what I was getting into, but in the moment, it felt like something Gabby would have done. She was a risk-taker when it came to running her business, and even though stuff wasn't ever perfect, it always worked out. I learned a lot from her about trusting my gut and even though, I had never planned on having my own dance company, I wasn't an idiot. This was an amazing opportunity that fell right into my lap.

It was such an in-my-face opportunity, it reminded me of my dad telling me to pick the stars that were the brightest and this couldn't get any brighter. I felt my lips stretching my cheeks so far, they got sore. For a girl who never had a career plan, things were falling into place. I was an entrepreneur. And the best kind because I could still work my full-time job with the theatre while honing my business. I covered my mouth with my hands, stifling a scream. Then I came up for oxygen, looked at Henry again, and asked, "Where do I sign?"

Chapter Nineteen

Transitioning the dance classes to my new studio was the easiest thing ever. All the girls were relieved to have a new dance home and even more thrilled that they got to stay together. I only had one minor hiccup and that was on the first day when I showed up for the early morning classes, and my key to access the top floor didn't work in the lock. Feeling the pressure to look professional for my first official day of being a dance company owner, I could feel a cold sweat build on my lower back. I immediately called Becky. "Hey, is there something up with the locks here? I can't get in."

"Oh, yes!" Becky said. "After we closed yesterday, I forgot to tell you that Henry changed the locks. My mom had told him it's always a good idea to change the locks after you've switched owners. I totally spaced that my mom sent over her locksmith to take care of everything yesterday. I'm so sorry!"

"Do you have a spare key?" I checked my watch, confirming I still had an hour before class was scheduled to start, but even with the extra time, I was feeling anxiety build in my chest.

"Henry must have your set, but he won't be in this early," she troubleshot out loud. "I have my set you can use, but this stinks so bad with the worst timing because I'd come drop it off, but my mom was double booked. I just agreed to sub for her on a million-dollar closing deal in New Jersey and I should have left a few minutes ago. I can't be late for it because it's a top client of hers, but I can leave my keys here at her office if you can run down."

"I'll have to," I said, starting to panic. Then we hung up and I ran fourteen blocks to Becky's mom's office. It was the first time I had ever been inside her office, and I immediately felt underdressed when I saw all the high-end designer suits and handbags. Vastly aware that I was walking into this environment with tights and leg warmers, I kept my chin tucked down as I headed to the receptionist's desk. Then I came out of the biggest brain freeze of my life and my feet cemented to the floor. I had completely forgotten that my mom worked here—and there she was!

I took a heart-protecting step back. Not because I had planned on it, but I was that startled to see her. My eyes latched onto hers and I froze as I had forgotten how beautiful she could be when she tried. The last couple of years, she had been on a downward spiral with her health, and all I ever noticed was her unibrow, but now that I was standing in front of her—made-up and dressed-up—as she played the role of a trusted receptionist at a luxury New York Real Estate company—it moved me to see her look like this because it made her look normal.

Then I reminded myself it was a façade. There was no way her perfect posture, new highlights, and black-rimmed spectacles could change who she was. It was an act, but *man did I want to believe it.* Running her hand through a lost strand of hair, she greeted me with straight lips. "Abs. How are you?"

"I'm good." It seemed like a simple reply—often it was used in passing to avoid further small talk— but to me, it was more than that. I had been through so many trials that she wouldn't begin to know about, and I was finally in a place in my life where I *was* good—no thanks to her.

"That's wonderful," she replied. "I have keys for you." She picked up a keyring from the back counter and placed them on the top counter in front of her. "Becky said you needed them."

I nodded. Then said, "Yeah, I'm renting." There was still always a tiny part of my heart—like the tiniest corner way down in the bottom tip—that still believed that maybe somewhere down in the deepest pit of her heart, she had to care to know about my life, and I added, "I opened my own dance studio."

Her face was steadfast, not confirming if she had already known that detail or not. I wasn't expecting her to be impressed because she had always hated my dancing, but this felt different. "That's nice," she said. Then I continued to deadpan, feeling a little stiff because she hadn't tried to initiate more conversation. I wished I could say it didn't bother me, but I hung my head when I turned to leave with my heart feeling like it had been stuffed full of lead. Even though she looked amazing, nothing had changed.

"Have a nice day," she said politely like I was any other random person who stopped in to pick up something. That stung because I wasn't any other person. I was her daughter. I fumbled for a goodbye appropriate to fit the situation, but I didn't want to say goodbye. I needed to because I had dancers arriving at my studio, but I had a moment of clarity. I had done so much work on my life by pushing myself. I felt like if I wanted to finish healing and forgive her completely, I needed to take the advice Wally had given me about learning to just love her because she was my mom but let go of everything else. I knew there was something I needed to do. I lifted my chin and said clearly, "I love you, Mom."

Her eyes grew wide but didn't soften and I held no expectation for her to say it back. I simply smiled, gave a soft wave, and left, not knowing when I'd see her again. But that tiny space I had reserved for her in my heart felt lighter and for that, it was worth it.

Running back to my studio at rocket pace, I victoriously made it in time to greet my first dancers. I don't think I heard a word anybody said to me because my head was up in clouds from my excitement. When the last dancer had left, and I was sweeping up my already meticulously shined floor, I heard chatter and footsteps coming back up the stairs, then Becky and Wally appeared in my doorway with their arms affectionately hooked into each other's. "How'd it go?" Becky asked, pulling her smile so tight, it looked like she wanted to squeal.

"Amazing! I don't know why I never thought about having a dance company before. Now that it's mine, I have so many ideas for everything, from the leotards to productions. I am going to do everything princess I can and everything super girly."

"Oh, I'm so glad," Becky exclaimed, then lowered her voice. "I'm sorry about this morning. I totally forgot about the key thing."

"It's okay. It worked out."

Wally pointed to the door where I had placed a sign with my newly revealed dance company logo. "How'd you come up with the name Bright Star Studio?"

I lowered my eyes because up until now it had been my secret. "It's something my dad used to talk about. Like, when I was lost, he'd tell me you don't have to know where you're going. Just pick the brightest star and move toward it."

"Ah," Becky cooed. "I love that."

My lips curled and I looked heavenward when I said, "Thanks. I do too."

"So, now that the big first day is over. What are your plans for tonight?" Wally asked.

"Nothing really. It's finals week for Fulton, so I probably won't even see him," I reminded them. "And then graduation this weekend, so that'll be fun."

"That's right." He bobbed his head, and the smile on his face was fully supportive. "I bet he's excited."

"I think part of him is," I said, then added, "You

know him. He can't live in the moment with that stuff, so of course he's already started checking out his textbooks for next year and trying to look at different apartments online, getting ready for the next act."

"Are you serious?" Wally's jaw dramatically dropped. "He needs to knock it off and go celebrate. He can be a worrywart later."

"You can tell him that because he won't listen to me."

He pulled his phone out, saying, "I'll call him right now."

Before he could dial, I put my hand up to stop him. "Well, don't call now. He's got a final in an hour and I know he'll be cramming. But you can call in a couple of hours."

"That's kind of sad," Becky said. "You both have two amazing things going on this week and you don't have any plans to celebrate?"

"I guess not." I shrugged, adding, "We've been so busy, I don't think we had time to think about it."

"You'd better let us at least take you out for dinner," Becky insisted. "It's too special not to commemorate."

"Not tonight. Fulton won't have time because he'll want to study for tomorrow's final."

"What about Sunday then after graduation?" Wally asked.

I grimaced. I hated having to say no, but I knew his parents were going to be in town, and I didn't think he'd want to ditch them. "I can ask him, but he's going to be busy with family."

"I see how it is," he joked but his voice held an edge

that made me feel like he wasn't seeing the humor in it as he went on, "He's going to move to Florida and forget about his friends and have his nose up in the air because he's a big-time grad school student."

Shooting him the lamest look I could, I started to wonder if he was intentionally trying to make me feel bad. "Where are you going with this?"

"Nowhere. I was just wondering what the plan was."

"There really isn't a plan. He's not moving yet. Griz hired him to work at the restaurant over the summer. He thought it would be a good way to save a lot of money and get to stay in the city a little longer. Then he'll move in August sometime."

Wally arched an eyebrow at me. "And you're going to stay here and have the dance studio?"

Becky cut in, "Honey, you're sounding sort of nosey."

"It's okay." I figured the reason he was prying was to see if I had plans to quit my job. I wanted to assure him I was committed to working for him. "Yeah, I'm excited about what we can do next year. I have big plans for a huge Christmas ballet colab." He didn't say anything, so I added, "I thought last year was busy, but I think this year is going to be even crazier. I won't even have time to think about Fulton being in Florida." I hoped that would be enough to convince Wally that I wasn't going to bail on him.

Then Becky turned to Wally. "I don't think this is working. Can you give me a minute with her alone?" He agreed and before I could ask about what wasn't working, he left, leaving Becky and me alone. She turned back to me. "Sorry if that felt like an interrogation. Wally's not asking about your job." She stopped, letting her eyes hit mine. "Truthfully," she added, "I was worried about you, thinking about how hard it's going to be with Fulton being gone. You never talk about it, and I had asked him if you had said anything to him. I know it's weird. Sorry."

"It'll be fine. We've done long distance before." I stubbornly reassured her as I looked away. Becky stood biting her lip, not saying anything, so I said, "I'll go visit him when he gets breaks from school and we'll talk every day on the phone."

"It doesn't have to be this way." Becky's voice was soft, and even though she was vague, I knew exactly what she was referring to, and I shook my head. She wasn't going to convince me. She continued, "Fulton wants you to come with him. This is dumb that you can't go be with him. You love each other."

I fanned both my hands out in front of me to reference the studio I was standing in. "I can't move to Florida. I just opened a dance studio."

"Its temporary. You can make it work." I didn't say anything, so she added, "It's too important not to."

"How am I going to run a dance studio in New York if I'm living in Florida?"

"Most of the stuff you do, you can do online. If you need an on-site coordinator, I'm here." She pointed down the hall. "I'm moving into the apartment in a couple months, so I'm literally right here all the time. It's not a big deal if you need me to make sure everything's locked up at night or I can do whatever."

She touched my arm lightly, then said, "I'm here for you."

"I couldn't expect you to do that because you already have two jobs and you're not going to want to mess with this too."

"You're making an excuse . . ."

"I'm not."

"Let me help you. It's a few years. You can come back as needed to run the show. The studio will be waiting for you when Fulton's done with vet school. It's perfect."

"Psh. In a fairy tale." My voice was noticeably growing in discontentment.

"Why not?" She pressed. "Why won't you at least talk to Fulton about it?"

I shook my head and took a defensive step backward. "I couldn't do that."

"You won't talk to him because he'll think it's a great idea."

"Why are you doing this to me?" Becky was never confrontational in anything she did. She was forever the people-pleaser and this was so out of character for her that it was blowing my mind more than her stupid accusations.

She looked away, like she was going to give up, but she surprised me with the biggest blow of her mouth ever. "You're not your mom."

Now I knew she didn't look away because she was giving up; she looked away to give me space to talk about my mom, but I didn't want to. "Stop it."

"Abs."

"Stop it," I said a little firmer.

"You have to talk about it."

"No!" I screamed, getting in her face. "Are you happy? Now I'm mad."

"Good," she said firmly. "You need to get mad. She's awful to you." I double blinked my eyes in shock. Becky had never uttered a bad word about my mom even in high school when we both prided ourselves on being mean girls. I thought she was done, but she went on, "I've kept my mouth shut, telling myself you'll figure it out, but you didn't. Then you started seeing that counselor and I told myself she'd help you, but I don't know that it's working because you're still making the same mistakes. I can't watch you do this anymore."

"Do what?" I fumbled.

"Hurt like this."

"I'm fine."

She ignored my rebuttal and calmly said, "Your mom was never a mom." I felt my eyebrows fall and tighten. Then Becky said, "She never showed any signs of support or love." My lungs twisted, sealing up my airways, but Becky continued, "She let you down so many times and buried your self-esteem in the mud."

"Stop it."

"Am I wrong?" she argued back. "Am I?"

"No," I bit back. "You're right, but why are you doing this?"

"Because you're not her! You're not going to be like her! Your mom did all those things because she is sick. But you know what else?"

"What?" I angrily perched a hand on my hip and stuck my chin out.

"You're not like your mom, but you are like your dad."

I winced, not wanting to bring my dad into this.

"Who learned how to sub as a pyramid base for cheerleading so you could get extra practice on week-ends being a flyer?" My lips parted, stunned she even remembered how I had wanted to beat out Erica for that position, so I begged him to help me, and it had worked. Before I had time to linger more on the memory, she spouted, "Who watched all those YouTube videos to learn how to French braid your hair so we could have matching hairdo's at school? Who pulled you out of school and lied saying you were sick the day you got ditched by your Snowball date?"

"He pulled us both out of school," I corrected her. I could feel my heartbeat grow stronger, reminding me I was human.

"Yeah, and took us for ice cream and—"

"To see the Rockettes." I blinked tears back and snapped, "So?"

"So, you're not your mom!" She screamed so close to me, I wanted to punch her to get her out of my face, but before I could, she lowered her voice. "But you are *so* your dad's daughter, and you can love just as fierce as he did—if you'd only allow it." She dramatically crossed her arms across her chest and turned away letting out a disgruntled "huff."

Her words rang around in my head, refeeding my brain over and over. I started to see them repeat and stack up into a huge list, a list so long it wrapped up like a scroll. "You're not your mom. You're not your mom. You're not your mom, etc." I always touted my imagination because it aided me in my creativity, but in this moment, I hated how visual my mind made things. I could close my eyes or yell at them to stop, but it wouldn't have worked. Rolling words spun in my brain.

Then I heard Becky ask, "In a perfect life where nothing else mattered—the job, the money, your mom, nothing, and Fulton gets on a plane to move to Florida, would you want to go?"

Then my brain cleared, the repeating words drying up. I followed Becky's question and gave myself permission to push my job out of my brain, and the money and my mom and then there was Fulton left, but I couldn't push him out of my mind. I shook my head, a little disgusted because her question was dumb. "Well, when you say it like that, who wouldn't go?"

"You aren't."

"Because life doesn't work like that."

"Because you don't let it, but you just admitted you *want* to go."

My heartbeat slowed in retreat. *I did just admit it.* I felt a widening of my perception, like I was being lifted and given a bird's eye view. *I want to go with Fulton.* In my view from above, I could see a fear that had strangled me up like an ugly root and its trap had left me petrified, thinking that I wouldn't be enough for Fulton because I was my mother's child. My eyes had been opened. This scene was over. *But I have one scene left . . .*

Chapter twenty

Just like the principal in a narrative ballet, I instantly knew the sequence I needed to perform. I fumbled around for my winter coat, and ran out the door, leaving Becky standing there wondering, and hopped a train to Stony Brook. "Biochemistry," I repeated to myself while I walked briskly through the campus courtyard. "He said he had a Biochemistry final." I had never spent any time on a college campus other than the handful of times I had met Fulton here, so I had no idea where to go. I scanned the buildings like I was looking for a flashing neon sign that said, "Biochemistry Final in Here," but there wasn't such a sign. "Center for Arts," I read out loud as I ran past a building that was obviously not Chemistry. Starting to feel like my plan was a bad plan, I anxiously scanned both sides of the street and kept running. I was about to stop someone to ask how people know where to go, but then I finally saw a building with the word Chemistry and I cried out a celebratory, "Yes!"

As I scurried up the sidewalk, students started to pour out the door. Some of them carried gray textbooks, that I had recognized to be like the one I had seen in Fulton's dorm room. *That was his book! This was his chemistry class!* I stretched my neck to see over the wave of students. Checking each face didn't help because soon the students slowed to a trickle and eventually stopped. I never saw Fulton. I spun on my heel, to go back in the other direction, thinking I had somehow passed him and I got halfway down the block again when I heard his voice call after me, "Abs?"

Spinning around again, I wanted to run into his arms with a smile on my face, but instead the moment I saw him, my eyes were pierced with a sting and I broke into tears. He quickly ran to me and pulled me into an embrace. "What happened?" he demanded.

I shook my head, trying to tell him that nothing had happened and that I was fine, but it wouldn't come out because the truth was that *everything* had happened. I had gotten a new perspective on our relationship and now I was terrified I was too late.

"You're scaring me," Fulton said as he kept trying to tuck his face down to see my own face as I continued to bury it further into his chest. "What happened?"

I didn't know how to begin to explain what had happened to me in the last couple of hours. Then it became clear that it didn't matter what *had* happened. That was my history, and I was done living in the past.

All that mattered was what happened next. "I lied to you," I blurted out.

His eyes grew wide at first but then narrowed. "About what?"

I arched my head back to look at him and sniffed before saying, "Everything."

"Everything," he echoed, his voice grew on edge. "That's a little vague."

"It's all a lie," I fumbled for words, but then got my verbal footing and started to ramble, "I lied when I said we'd be okay doing the long-distance relationship because I don't want to do that."

His face flushed, and his forehead stacked with worry lines, but before he could speak, I continued, "I lied to myself. I said it's what I wanted, but it wasn't. I didn't think I'd be enough for you, and I didn't want to make you give up on your dreams for me, but that's not fair for me to lie because you need to know that I do want to be with you. I don't want to stay here without you. I hate the idea of you living so far away." I stopped talking and sucked in a bunch of air before I got lightheaded.

"I'm confused . . ." His forehead still held his worry lines, but his eyes were starting to gleam with a sparkle.

"I want to come with you to Florida and if you promise not to make a big fuss about it, I want to get married."

I wish I could remember what Fulton said next, but my heart was beating too loud against my eardrums, and all the words faded into the background. I know I stood frozen, my heart all exposed, but I didn't regret it

217

because just like in a romantic ballet, he wrapped an arm around my waist and spun me closer until our lips met in a kiss. Then I giggled to myself, thinking this was one heck of a grand finale.

But no good ballet is without an encore. Mine was silent but so sweet.

When the night was quiet, and I had arrived home, I slid through my apartment door, careful not to stir Becky. The light from her bedroom glowed out the bottom of her door, but tonight I smiled, knowing she was still talking to Wally. My eyes grazed the mail on the counter, and I found a package with my name on it.

It wasn't my birthday, but I knew this little square box had to be special after the day I had lived. A hand-written note from my aunt Kim scribbled about how this item was the only thing recovered in the rubble of my mom's scourged condo. She had tried to call to ask if I wanted it, but missed me, so she sent it.

I didn't know how he planned it so perfectly timed, but I knew it was his design when I pulled out a preserved Yankees mug. Not just any mug, but this one was special because the logo had accidentally been printed on the wrong side, making it ideal for a left-handed person like my dad. It had been his gripe that they didn't make mugs for left-handed people. When he found this mistake, he hailed it was because not only was the mug meant for him, but the Yankees were calling him to work for them. The thing was that my dad was an expert marketer and won every campaign he ever tried to get—except for the Yankees, but he never gave up. And even though they were always just out of reach, he never counted it as a failure because he insisted that unless you had something to reach for, your passion would dry up. I clenched his mug in my hands, holding it close to my heart. I knew this was his blessing and said, "Thanks, Dad."

Chapter Twenty One

The following week, Fulton surprised me at work with a train ticket to the beach and a picnic basket lunch. It wasn't warm outside, but that didn't stop us from making the trip to Long Island. I thought the picnic was the whole surprise but after we ate, Fulton put on his serious face, drawing my eyes to his when he said, "I was thinking about last week when you came to campus and told me you wanted to come with me to Florida."

"What about it?" I could feel my cheeks start to pre-heat because I still couldn't believe I had been that vulnerable.

"I was so surprised to see you that I sort of feel like everything was rushed and something about what we agreed upon is bothering me."

His gaze was fixed on me, sending an alarm right to my heart, which instantly felt like an accordion starting to fold and deflate. "What are you talking about?"

"It bothers me when I think back on these last few months and all the raw conversations we had to have to get to that point, and it was so hard—"

"Are you kidding me?" My hand fled to cover my breaking heart because I could totally tell he was backing out on me now.

"Stop." He grabbed my now trembling hand back and pulled it in close to his chest. "Stop for a minute. It's not bad. I promise." The smile he gave me seemed to etch a softness in my heart that I was needing in that moment, so I trusted and waited while he continued, "I think about those little hard moments and talks we went through now, and I'm grateful for them because even though at one point I thought it might be hopeless, it all worked out and I think we are stronger because of it, but the thing that is bothering me is . . . I've been lying to you about something else." My withered heart dropped an inch in my chest, beating hard and fast like a drum as I now froze, glaring a Fulton as I waited for him to explain. "So, something else that I never told you, but I hope you understand, is that I've mentioned before that I went to see your dad before he died."

I could feel the color drain from my face, wondering why he would bring this up now. Sucking in my bottom lip, I trusted he had a point because he had just promised me that whatever he was going to tell me wasn't bad, but it was getting harder to stay quiet while he continued, "You see, I knew already then that I wanted to marry you and I couldn't lose the opportunity to ask your dad, out of respect. So, that trip I took to see your dad was really about asking for your hand in marriage, but I knew you weren't ready and that's the real reason I kept that a secret from you."

My voice snagged in the back of my throat, and a veil that I didn't even know was there, was suddenly dropped. "What did he say?" My voice cracked from weakness.

Fulton's lips rolled in, and it was obvious that was a hard memory for him. I didn't even need him to say it because I knew my dad loved Fulton like a son. "He said I had his blessing."

It was then that I caught Fulton with the softest gaze I'd ever seen on his face, and he seemed to see right through me. Then he used his free hand and pulled something out of his pocket. I didn't have to look at it, to know what it was. Closing my eyes, I willed my brain to imprint this moment forever inside it. When I opened my eyes, I saw Fulton take a knee, and with the ring pinched between his index finger and thumb, he fixed his eyes on mine. "It bothers me that we never had this moment because you deserve a proper proposal."

I wanted to blurt out yes so fast, but I could see on his face that as much as he wanted me to have this moment, he also wanted it. So, with every ounce of restraint, I bit my lip hard and listened. He tilted his head slightly to the side, flashing me my favorite heart-stopping look. "Aubergine, will you marry me?"

The tears beat my words, pouring out like a freaking Nigra Falls and the harder I tried to fight them, the more my words stayed glued in my chest. I had been waiting for the last two minutes with an eager yes on the tip of my tongue, but now that it was finally my turn to speak, all I could do was nod like an out-of-control bobblehead. Leaning in closer to me, I could tell Fulton was waiting for my words, and *finally* I broke through my tears and managed a breathless, "yes."

Weak in the knees, I waited for him to slip the ring on my finger. Then he stood back up, lifting me off the ground with him. I couldn't wait another moment and leaned in, kissing him like I couldn't stand not to. Our lips locked together like they were sharing secrets and I knew in that instant I was undeniably forever fused with him. My heart was overtaken with a new conviction that whatever happened after now, Fulton and I would face it together and that was one thousand trillion percent the way it was supposed to be. The journey we took to here was a flipping mini-series, but I knew that was what I had to do to get to this moment and for that I was forever grateful because I finally knew without a doubt that I had a heart that loved.

THE END

Also by J.P. Sterling

Other books written by J.P. Sterling

Water and Stone Duet

Ruby in the Water

Lily in the Stone.

A Heart that Dances Series

Dancing on Broken Ankles

The Stars We See

A Heart that Dances

A Heart that Loves

Releasing in 2023

Maid for my Billionaire Boss (A Sweet Romantic Comedy)

CPSIA information can be obtained
at www.ICGtesting.com
Printed in the USA
LVHW100444210622
721699LV00005B/196

9 780998 442167